Capitol Hill Library

JAN 24 2018

D0049621

NO LONGER PROPERTY OF
SEATTLE PUBLIC LIBRARY

The Off Season

The **Off** Season

Amy Hoffman

The University of Wisconsin Press

The University of Wisconsin Press
1930 Monroe Street, 3rd Floor
Madison, Wisconsin 53711-2059
uwpress.wisc.edu

3 Henrietta Street, Covent Garden
London WCE 8LU, United Kingdom
eurospanbookstore.com

Copyright © 2017 by Amy Hoffman
All rights reserved. Except in the case of brief quotations embedded in critical
    articles and reviews, no part of this publication may be reproduced, stored
    in a retrieval system, transmitted in any format or by any means—digital,
    electronic, mechanical, photocopying, recording, or otherwise—or
    conveyed via the Internet or a website without written permission of the
    University of Wisconsin Press. Rights inquiries should be directed to
    rights@uwpress.wisc.edu.

Printed in the United States of America

This book may be available in a digital edition.

Library of Congress Cataloging-in-Publication Data

Names: Hoffman, Amy, author.
Title: The off season / Amy Hoffman.
Description: Madison, Wisconsin: The University of Wisconsin Press, [2017]
Identifiers: LCCN 2017010432 | ISBN 9780299314606 (cloth: alk. paper)
Subjects: LCSH: Lesbians—Fiction. | Provincetown (Mass.)—Fiction.
    | LCGFT: Novels.
Classification: LCC PS3608.O47738 O34 2017 | DDC 813/.6—dc23
LC record available at https://lccn.loc.gov/2017010432

To
Provincetown

Contents

Contents

The Vortex

The year Janelle and I moved to Provincetown—for her to heal and grow stronger, for me to paint my masterpiece, for the two of us to mend our bruised relationship—was the year I became a cad. Janelle, with her scientific mind, would tell you it was because I introduced an uncontrolled variable into our experiment—that is, Baby Harris—so of course it didn't produce the anticipated results, as if anything does. Although I did do a lot of painting. But in Brooklyn, I had been a nice person. Or maybe I'm deluded. That would be Janelle's interpretation. Maybe I always had it in me.

Provincetown was always a crucial element in the Janelle-and-Nora story, even before we decided to move there. Picture Cape Cod: a raised arm, biceps pumped, elbow crooked, fingers curled under. The loose fist encircles Provincetown and its small, incongruous population of writers, visual artists, spiritual seekers, drag queens, regular queens, lesbians, Portuguese former fisherfolk ("former" because their livelihoods were largely destroyed by overfishing and climate change), Yankee drunks, miscellaneous nonconformists, and Margot, an extraordinary personage who embodied, busking on the street in a leather miniskirt with a handmade placard that read "70 Years Young, Living My Dream," all of the above at once. If you drove out to the tip of the Cape on Route 6, which runs right down the middle of the long peninsula, the place felt like the end of the line. But if you could look down on it from above, like the gulls and pigeons do, you would see that it is, rather, the center of a vortex, the currents of ocean and bay swirling around it—concentrating the forces of imagination, desire, and precarious natural beauty.

Janelle and I met there, in the eye of the vortex, cute. It was high summer, and I was on a bike, pumping up the hill on Bradford Street that runs alongside the high school parking lot, my hand out to signal a left onto Carver, when another cyclist plowed into me from behind. Fortunately, because of the crowds, none of the cars was moving very fast, and neither were those of us on bicycles. I went over in slow motion.

"Sorry, sorry, sorry, sorry, oh my God!" the other cyclist cried out, jumping off her bike and gathering up the library books that had fallen off my rear rack. "I guess I got distracted!"

At first I was less angry than terrified by being knocked into traffic. Struggling to guide the bike onto the sidewalk, I realized the handlebars were now facing one way and the front wheel another. The tire was flat. My knee was bleeding. "I hate the way people drive around here!" I shouted. "Shit! Fuck! Piss! Why can't you watch where you're going?"

She handed me the books, so now I had to manage those with one arm while wheeling my crazy bike with the other. "I'm so sorry!" she repeated, trailing after me. "This has never happened to me before! Let me help you with your bike!"

"It's not my bike. It's a rental," I said. "Go away."

When I finally succeeded in dragging the bike back to the shop, the guys were amazingly unsympathetic, despite my bloody knee and all, and I had to have a big argument with them about returning my security deposit.

That evening I saw her again, sitting on one of the benches outside Spiritus Pizza, eating a slice and watching the vacationing hoards charging up and down Commercial Street. She was short and stocky and dark skinned, her hair in short dreadlocks. "Hey!" Janelle waved me over. "It's you! Are you okay?"

I showed her the bandage I had wrapped around my knee.

"Looks painful," she said.

"It is," I said. "You idiot."

"I'm usually so careful," she said. "I'm truly sorry. I got distracted."

"Oh, forget it," I said, noticing her dimples. "Maybe I'll end up with an intriguing scar."

"Want a slice?" she asked. "I'm buying tonight. Greek or cheese?"

"Greek," I said. "So what distracted you, anyway?" On Commercial, I could have understood it—the crowds, the views of the harbor—but on Bradford it's all traffic and straight couples dragging their kids up the hill.

"You," said Janelle, standing up from the bench.

"First you nearly kill me," I said. "Now you're embarrassing me."

She went inside to the counter to order our pizza. When she returned, she continued, "You have very well-defined calf muscles."

"I do?" I said.

"Don't fish," she said. "Yes, you do. I like that on a girl." She handed me my slice. "Are you here by yourself? I am."

"I'm with friends. They've been inviting women over for dinner all week, but—"

"Uh-huh. You do better on your own," she said. "You caught me, girl."

So that's how it started.

The way she came on to me, I thought she was looking for a simple vacation hookup—which I was excited to experience, since I had never been much good at keeping things casual. I was the serial monogamy type. With, I admit, lapses. But being lesbians—rather than gay men, such as, for example, Janelle's friend Roger, who became my friend too, at least for a time, and who didn't like to learn even the real names of his tricks, although he would tolerate a *nom d'amour* like Blake or Lancelot or Crusher—Janelle and I started talking: basic biographical information; first love; daring sexual practices and venues (frottage to orgasm on the lawn at Tanglewood; handcuff play in girlfriend's sister's apartment, with girlfriend's sister banging on the door). When we got as far as exchanging addresses, we discovered we lived in the same neighborhood. So much for same-time-next-year. I was renting a one-bedroom I could no longer afford since she-who-shall-not-be-named had moved out six months before, while just a few blocks away, Janelle owned a huge renovated loft, with a spare room that she had always meant to make into a workshop but that was currently serving as storage for her exercise equipment.

"You're right," I said when she showed me around. "This would make a great studio. South-facing, good light." Janelle gave me a big wet kiss, and we made love on her yoga mat. It wasn't quite a lesbian-second-date/U-Haul situation, but it was close.

The Gravitron Starship 4000

I hadn't understood at first that my sweet Janelle was a genius, literally. In math, she had vacuumed up every prize her department had to offer. Since graduate school, though, she had moved away from abstraction. What she really loved was tinkering, figuring out how things worked. She once built herself a computer. From a kit, for fun. That's what she told me, "fun." It took her a couple of weekends; it would have taken me all my life and then some: around and around, chained to the everlasting karmic wheel, damned to finish my hardware. She had created a successful consulting practice developing software systems for small businesses, in which she tried to keep her relationships with her clients, as much as possible, virtual. "It's neater that way," she explained to me. "If I don't know their stories, I don't have to feel guilty about what I'm charging them." Because when people met Janelle, they told her things. It was the way she listened, as though she had never before heard anything so fascinating. And in fact her interest was absolutely genuine, and once she learned what you were up to, she couldn't stop herself from getting involved. From tinkering. Her clients adored her.

My own unstable income was hacked together with scotch tape and string: adjunct gigs, a private student or two, some gallery sitting, occasionally a commission, once or twice a prize, and the rare, miraculous sale. But Janelle never minded that. "I'm a patron of the arts," she would say, just really pleased about it.

So I was kept, at least partly, and less than pleased about it, but I tried to repress all that. Because Janelle made me happy—and I made

5

her happy, too; she's never denied that. We had friends, we went out dancing and to movies and dinner parties and plays, and we were busy, busy, busy, like all New Yorkers, I with my art, she with her computers and whatnot—I never exactly understood what she did, as many times as she patiently tried to explain it.

Even our racial difference didn't seem to get in the way. At most, it was grist for illuminating comparisons and discussion, a little healthy friction—perhaps because despite it, our backgrounds were so similar: Both of us from the striving middle classes of the boroughs, Brooklyn for me, Queens for her. Parents who were teachers and social workers, uncles who were dentists, aunts who were their bookkeepers. Exam schools: Music and Art, Bronx Science. A decade after we first bashed into each other, we still had sex once or twice a week. Other couples told us we were their role models.

We were so lucky, for so long.

There has to be an "*until . . . ,*" right?

Until Janelle got cancer.

She always hated getting mammograms. I mean, no one likes it, but she had a near phobia. Still, she would take half a valium and go when it was time, and then it would be over for another year. Except once.

"It hurt more than ever," she told me when she got home. I would have made her a comforting cup of tea, because that's what I would have wanted, but Janelle hated tea, which she said looked to her like dirty water, so I brewed her a shot of coffee in her special espresso machine. She liked to drink that night and day; she said it helped her think. And sleep—she maintained that a coffee at the right time at night knocked her right out. Go figure. I said her espresso wasn't dirty water; it was mud. *Good swamp mud!* Janelle used to growl.

We sat down next to each other on the living room couch, where we reconnoitered each evening, and where we had our most important conversations. We called it our Honesty Couch—which is just so sweet, isn't it? "I'm still aching," she said.

"Aw, baby," I said, putting my arm around her and pulling her toward me. "Come here and let me kiss it and make it better."

"No, don't," she said, pushing me away. "You don't understand. I have a bad feeling."

After that, every step of the way, when they called her back for another scan, for an ultrasound, for a biopsy—when we made the appointment with the fucking surgeon!—I became more and more resistant. "You don't know, honey. They make mistakes all the time. It's probably just a cyst, like I always get, remember?" My doctor had told me I had a condition called "dense breast tissue," which I thought didn't sound like a condition at all, just normal human breasts, but the doctor claimed it made my tests difficult to read, and I often had to return for multiple sessions. "Wait until we really understand what's going on."

At first, Janelle actually found my nonsense reassuring. "You're right, you're right," she would say. "I'll try to calm down."

"That's right, honey. Breathe."

She would have been better off buttonholing the mail carrier or some other random person on the street. I don't like to admit this, but basically, I'm not the woman you want by your side in an emergency. It's not simply denial: I get stupid. I've actually felt my thought processes slowing down, until whatever's just happened can't penetrate my seized-up brain, and I'm running in circles, flapping my arms around. Not effective. You're much better off with someone like Janelle, who gets revved up and superenergized in times of trouble and starts doing ten things at once. All of them splendidly.

"Black women have a much worse prognosis than whites," she told me one evening. "Did you know that? Even us well-educated, well-paid sisters with health insurance. I've been researching this."

Of course she had. "I told you to stop it!" I yelled, displaying yet again my wondrous powers of denial. "Prognosis. Why are you jumping to that already? You don't even have a *diag*nosis."

"Why are you yelling at me?"

"I don't know. I—because maybe it's nothing, Janelle!"

She bristled. "Nothing to you. Even if it's just some idiot's finger-print on the X-ray, it's not nothing. It's the environment. Look at where we live! Brooklyn! The Gowanus Canal is practically a Superfund site. People have been dumping shit into it since, I don't know, 1800 or some-thing. Cancer's probably in the air, in the dust—in the dirt! And we wanted a vegetable garden—how stupid can you get?"

"Don't say *cancer*," I said.

"Don't be superstitious. It's a word."

The trick of the Gravitron Starship 4000 carnival ride is to whirl around so fast that revelers find themselves stuck to the walls by cen-trifugal force. Then the floor folds away. I was sitting next to Janelle in her doctor's office when he told her the results of her biopsy, and I felt a Gravitron-like vertigo as we were slammed into a new space-time gov-erned by wacko physical rules. He was referring her to an oncologist, the carpeted floor dropping away beneath our feet. That night, we held each other in bed, and looking back, it seems to me that all we said to each other in the darkness was "*Cancer*."

"Cancer."

"*Cancer*."

"Cancer."

Later, after that night, she was, most of all, angry. Not grief-stricken or immobilized or frightened, as I was, but simply furious. She couldn't sit still; she kept jumping up and stomping around the apartment. "I don't know what to do with myself, Nora! Lump-ectomy! It's the stupid-est term for a surgery I ever heard in my life; it's not even Latin!"

"It's not even pig-Latin!" I said, and that made her laugh at herself, for a moment.

"It's an embarrassment, to have an operation like that."

The Good Healer

Nevertheless, Janelle's lumpectomy went well, if such a thing can be said of such a surgery: she was, the oncologist said, a "good healer."

I was not a good healer. That was Roger. It's not like Janelle would have died without him, even if I sometimes felt that way. After all, she was only—that's what the doctors always said, *only*—stage one. *Very treatable*: they said that too. But Roger taught me how to care for her. He showed me what to do with the bandages and drains, and he encouraged her to eat and go for walks. He told me to go with her to her doctor appointments, to make a list of questions, to bring a pad and pen, to take notes. He knew the importance of an extra blanket in the late afternoon, a new pair of pajamas, a glass of water, a gentle touch. He could read Janelle's mood—when she was up for a visit from a friend, when she would rather have that person stay out of her way.

More and more, the person she would rather have stay out of her way was me. As much as Roger tried to teach me, I couldn't seem to develop the touch. I brought Janelle dinner on a tray, and she said the food was tasteless. I put a vase of flowers by her bed, and the scent made her choke. When I gave her a book, she said she was too exhausted to read anything but *Essence*. When I tried giving her a massage, she complained that I was poking her.

I was standing at the kitchen sink rinsing off a bunch of kale for a healthy new recipe Roger was showing me, and I asked him. "You're an elementary school teacher, not a nurse. How'd you learn to do all this?"

"Just call me Cherry Ames!" he said, turning away from me to lift the lid from a pot of rice we had put up to simmer. "You know," he said. "AIDS." He gave the rice a stir. "I think you'll need to soak those greens, doll. They're full of such good vitamins, and Janelle won't eat them if they're gritty."

She didn't simply say "dirt" anymore; she said, "cancer-dirt."

I should have asked Roger, *tell me more*, but I couldn't, at that point, take in anything else, or think of anyone but Janelle, and what was happening to her, and to us.

I was teaching that semester, and one afternoon, toward the end of her chemotherapy, I came home from class to find her curled in a fetal position in our bed, fully dressed, the curtains drawn against the sun, the room stuffy and dark. Trying not to wake her, I sat down carefully beside her and rested my hand on her shiny scalp, a touch she had found comforting at one time, and she cried out, "Oh! Don't!"

Startled, I jumped up. "Okay," I said. "I don't know what you want. I don't know what to do. You hate tea. You hate food. You hate being touched. You tell me."

"I'm just tired," she said into the pillow. "Just leave me alone." I stood staring at her for a while, but she didn't say anything else, and, wishing I had Roger's intuition, I left the room and called him.

"Well, obviously you should have gotten into bed too, Nora, and held her," he said, sounding as fed up with me as Janelle was. But I didn't think he had the right answer, either. He hadn't heard her shriek.

Everyone expects chemotherapy to be awful, and it was, in all the usual and unusual ways—nausea, exhaustion, strange fevers and itches, strange dreams and delusions—and when it was over, we celebrated, Janelle and Roger and me. He bought champagne and a huge bouquet of flowers, and we toasted over the peonies. Janelle and I had a brief, sunny interlude, with even a couple of mornings of slow, gentle loving. Her hair started to come in, although differently, gray and tufty, and she put away her scarves and baseball caps. Secretly I grieved for her dreadlocks.

Then she started radiation treatments, and they were almost worse than what had gone before. I had organized my schedule so that I could accompany her to the clinic every morning, but when I told her my plan, she wouldn't hear of it. From the very first visit, she went by herself. And although some people bond with their fellow sufferers, she refused to speak to the other patients, and spoke only when spoken to by the nurses and technicians. In the waiting room she read physics texts and worked British-style crossword puzzles, and at home she spent her afternoons e-mailing her old clients and putting her business back together. "I have to do this," she insisted through gritted teeth, when I begged her to slow down, to take a nap or a walk around the block. "It's not like *you're* going to support us, right?"

Right.

Although really that wasn't the point. The point was Janelle proving to herself she had survived, with her abilities and faculties intact. We made no toasts when she finished those treatments. In fact, she didn't announce that they had ended, and I realized it only because she stopped running out each morning to her appointment.

I know, I know, it's natural to vent your feelings on the people closest to you. But I was losing faith—in myself, in Janelle, in the two of us. We had drifted so far apart, we were barely within hailing distance, and I was afraid the tide would never turn.

It did, though—slowly. One spring morning, Janelle, who had always been an early riser, woke me with coffee in bed. I propped myself up on the pillows, and she sat down next to me and turned off my alarm.

"Hey, thanks," I said cautiously. "How kind."

"I want to be kind," she said.

"You haven't not been . . ."

She took the cup from me, put it on the nightstand, and took my hand in her cold one. "You're warm," she said.

"The coffee."

"I've been such a bitch."

"Don't say *bitch*," I said, a little shocked. It was not a word she ever used, and I had seen her shut down others for using it. "You had cancer."

"A total, barking bitch," she repeated. "And you tried to be so good to me, I realize that. I want to do better, Nora. I can't live like this. I don't want to be cold and resentful. It's not me." Her eyes filled—and Janelle was never a fluent crier, even after her diagnosis, when anyone would have excused a few tears. They gave no relief, she said, so why bother?

"I know that, honey," I said, and we started hugging and kissing, and even playing around a little, as the coffee on the night table got cold, and after that, we started to draw closer, and we resumed talking on our Honesty Couch in the evenings, and our life together seemed to be returning to the way it had been in the period we had started to call Before—except that the more Janelle tried to convince me that during the worst days of her illness I had not been clumsy and intrusive but on the contrary gentle and comforting, the more depressed I became. I didn't believe her—because in fact, she was wrong. I had never succeeded in making her better.

That August, the city air became so stifling and heavy that breathing it didn't feel like breathing air; it felt like huffing an actual substance, composed of truck exhaust and smog and the sweat of angry pedestrians. I had intended to spend the month as usual, madly trying to prepare my classes and to finish the projects I had started back in June, when the summer months had stretched out before me like a deserted beach, with an infinity of choices about where to plant my umbrella. But I got stuck.

I think it was the collage. I was working with tweezers and tiny pieces of paper that kept curling up and floating away, and little beads that rolled off the table and disappeared. One morning I went into my studio as usual, and a breeze, such as hadn't puffed through the window since the middle of June, and which there had been no reason to anticipate before September, had blown the whole thing into a pile of confetti. I couldn't bear the thought of sweeping it up and reassembling it. Instead, I sat down in my reading chair, and that's where Janelle found me when she came home that evening. I hadn't moved all day; it seemed pointless.

"Are you sick?" she asked, laying a cool, gentle hand on my forehead.

I shook my head. There was no point in discussing it, or anything, really. "This weather is rotten," I said. "When do you think it will break?"

"You're crying," said Janelle. "Oh my god. What's going wrong now? I thought we were going to be okay, but—"

"I'm not," I said, but I touched my face and realized she was right. "It's just sweat pouring down from this disgusting humidity."

She walked over to the work table and examined the remains of my piece.

"What I did on my summer vacation," I said.

"It's a midlife crisis," she concluded. "First me, now you."

"That's for guys. That's not my problem. And it absolutely wasn't yours. I just don't want to finish my picture. It's horrible here." I had lived in Brooklyn all my life, and I had never thought it was horrible. I liked it, with its rough style and hodgepodge of communities, and even as other townies cursed the artists and artisans who had begun trekking over the bridges to open galleries and gastropubs, I didn't mind them at all. I hadn't had to leave the neighborhood to find kindred spirits; I had just stayed put and they had come to me. But that day I began to wonder if, having lived my entire life within a geographic radius no wider than that of a primitive villager, I had a sort of urban agoraphobia.

Janelle, as though reading my thoughts, as she used to occasionally Before, coaxed me out of the studio and patted the space next to her on the Honesty Couch. "The answer is Provincetown," she said. "We need to get away from here."

"Too many bad experiences, too much bad shit."

"Exactly."

We sat together for hours that night, fantasizing, and then sketching out actual, practical plans. She would charge an outrageous rent for the loft, enough for us to live in a little house by the sea. She would take an office in town and consult; our little house would have an extra, sunny room for a studio, and I would paint. The move came together so quickly, we kept marveling that it must have been *meant to be*—whatever that means. We moved after Labor Day, and at first it really did seem like everything was falling into place for us, like Provincetown was the missing piece to our puzzle, the one that revealed the whole picture.

Trouble

For Janelle, the beach was for walking. Even in Province-town, surrounded by ocean and bay, she never went into the water, which she claimed did weird things to her hair. Even after she lost it all and it grew back and she started wearing it short, simple, and natural, she was just not in the habit. Instead, she liked to wander for miles, at dawn or at dusk, up and back, bending to pick up a rock, turning it over in her palm, skimming it out to sea. On our first morning, while I unpacked my studio, she found a flat, heart-shaped stone, gray, with a vein of white quartz slashing diagonally across the right auricle, and she placed it on the windowsill above the kitchen sink. Bless this home. She developed a knack for spotting sea glass, even the amber kind that comes from root beer bottles, which is rare, because how many people drink root beer to begin with, and then fling their bottles into the ocean? In the studio, I started fooling around with her finds, making some of them into jewelry.

It wasn't bad, either. I decided to take a booth at the annual Thanks-giving weekend craft fair at the Unitarian church. Venture into the community. My plan was to sell enough stuff to cover my share of the rent, which wasn't very practical—even I knew that. But I had begun to worry again about the financial imbalance between me and Janelle, and to wonder if it gave her an upper hand—not that a loving relationship is a competition or anything. Janelle sat me down and calculated that if I sold every trinket I had brought, I wouldn't clear more than a few hundred bucks. "But do what you need to do, sweetheart," she said, helping me load my stuff into the back of our car. "I've got us covered."

I fanned out a display of earrings, and next to the table I set up an easel with a portrait I had made of Janelle that had hung on our living room wall in Brooklyn. In it, she had round, dimpled cheeks and short dreadlocks tipped here and there with a bead or a cowrie shell. I had done her in a palette of affectionate browns and cinnamons and creams, against a background of that lovely apricot color you see on stucco houses in French villages. One of my more attractive works, I thought, even if she didn't exactly resemble it anymore, with her face so much thinner, her dimples more like hollows, her dreadlocks shorn. I propped a sign next to it: "Commissions Taken." At the last minute I had also dragged out a stack of the old art books I had inherited from my uncle. *Vintage*, was what I hoped the local artists would think, *cool*—but really the books were just dusty and outdated, the smell of wood pulp and mildew rising from the pages enough to choke any browser who took an interest and fanned them open.

So I set up my booth at the fair.

And Baby Harris walked in.

She stood for a moment in the doorway, scanning the room, then cut across the middle of it and walked right up to my table, and I thought, *Here comes trouble.* "I'm not looking for any," I said.

"Looking for any what?" said Baby.

"Any trouble," I said. "It's not what I'm looking for."

"Then you've come to the wrong woman," said Baby. "What's your name? Where have you been all my life?"

"Nora Griffin," I said, sticking out my hand. She took it and held it gently. Finally, I gave her hand a couple of firm shakes and pulled away.

"Ah, you're blushing, Nora Griffin," she said.

"Well, who wouldn't?" I said, flustered. "We just moved here a month ago. But I haven't been in here before. I'm new to the craft fair thing."

"*We* . . . ," Baby noted, glancing at the painting. She held one pair of earrings and then another to her cheek, and flipped through a fifties-era textbook on African sculpture. "'Primitive,'" she snorted and glared at me briefly, as though I were responsible for the author's colonialist attitude. "Nice bling, though. Do you have a card?"

I fumbled through my wallet and handed her one. It was soft around the edges. I hadn't often used them since we had arrived in Provincetown—or even back in Brooklyn, to be honest.

"I'll call," said Baby.

"No need for that," I said. "Just buy a pair now."

"Forgot my money," said Baby. She wiggled her fingers at me to say good-bye and strode back across the room. Who comes to the Unitarian church fair and doesn't bring cash? Not Baby. She stopped at the bake sale table, picked up a cupcake, put down a couple of bills, and wandered out, licking her fingers.

Superpowers

Baby was autumnal, all gold and vanilla. Thick hair, too long and tangled to be stylish; strangely dark, rough skin for a blonde—she said it was the Cape Cod sun, that it had left her permanently tanned, and it was true, I later discovered; you could see the outline of her swimsuit all winter long, across her chest and back, around her shoulders and thighs. Baby was tall and she looked her age and more. She had a bosom and a muffin top and a navel that plunged deep into her soft belly. Her brown eyes, if you caught them, gazed into yours more steadily and searchingly than she led you to expect from her flirtatious manner. She favored an unflattering shade of purpley-scarlet lipstick that no one could talk her out of and wore her red cowboy boots with everything—jeans, shorts, little black dresses. *Tak-tok-tak-tok.* You could hear Baby Harris coming and going.

Me, I was wintery. Black hair shot with silver, or rather, by then, silver shot with black. When you're in your twenties, your future projections don't include going gray—but there I was, for the first time in my life wearing blue, green, copper. Sea glass colors. By the ocean, I had decided to ditch my year-round Brooklyn black—no, I'll be honest. It wasn't the ocean; it was that I had had to buy new clothes. As Janelle had gotten thinner, I had filled out, finally, at age thirty-nine, developing a woman's hips and thighs. I had had to let go even of my favorite jacket, because the bottom button wouldn't close anymore. It was soft black velvet, the fabric of a puppeteer's overall, light-absorbing and invisible.

Supposedly women choose invisibility when asked whether they would prefer that or flight as a superpower—but not me. Not anymore. Who wouldn't prefer to fly? The water at the tip of the Cape was freezing and absolutely transparent; you could see your toes among the pebbles before you took your dive, and stroking through the waves really did feel a bit like flying. Not flying like the aerialist gulls, which swoop and glide without effort, but flying like the pigeons, which have to put some muscle into it, to push themselves through the gelid air.

"Janelle," I said as the chill settled in. "I've decided to swim during every single month of the year." Some of the year-rounders did it as a kind of spiritual, oneness-with-nature thing. I had overheard them talking about it in the checkout line at the Stop & Shop.

"White girls," said Janelle. "Uh-uh." She shook her head in feigned amazement. She said the year-rounders were nuts, and I was going nuts from listening to them.

My craft booth predictably hadn't worked out. No commissions—there were so many artists in Provincetown needing models that everyone already had more portraits, self-portraits, and busts of themselves than they knew what to do with. I had sold five pairs of earrings and a paperback, *The Letters of Vincent van Gogh*. Then the next day I woke up with an irresistible compulsion to read exactly that book, immediately, although I hadn't cracked it since my senior year of college. I had had to run out to borrow it from the library.

And a week later, just as I thought I had succeeded in putting my interesting encounter with Baby Harris out of my mind, she called. "What kind of name is that for an adult?" I asked obnoxiously, hoping, sort of, to put her off.

But she didn't seem to mind the personal question. "It's the only name I've ever had," she explained. "It's on my birth certificate. They were planning to come up with something else eventually, but Baby stuck."

"That's ridiculous," I said. "What were your parents thinking?"

"Now that," said Baby, "is something you don't want to know, Nora-dorable." There was a brief silence on the line, as she waited for me to flirt back. But I didn't respond. Somehow no one had ever come up with that particular endearment before. Baby continued cheerfully,

"Hey, are you trying to psychoanalyze me or something? I'll lie down on your couch any time."

"My couch." I wasn't ready for Baby on the couch. The you-know-what couch.

"Don't mind me," said Baby. "But I'm serious about the earrings. I want to see your stuff. I have a shop, you know. In addition, of course, to my fabulous personal collection of jewels."

So maybe it was just about a purchase, I thought. All the better. Maybe she would become a regular customer.

She should wear topaz, I thought. To match her eyes. Her knotted hair.

I flipped through the pages of *Van Gogh*, hoping it would sound through the phone line like I was searching my date book. "Can you come by at 3:15 on Friday?" I said officiously. "I think I can fit you in then." I could also have fit her in at 3:20, at 4:35, at 8:00 in the morning, whenever.

"Can't," said Baby—although I suspected that she, too, could have come any time. "How about now?"

When Baby showed up, she was all business. She quickly chose a pair of the amber sea glass earrings for herself, scooped up the rest of my creations for her store, placed an order for more, gave me a deposit, and left. *Tak-tok-tak-tok*, all the way down Commercial Street. I was disappointed. I was relieved.

That evening, Janelle came in from her walk with three more shards of the amber glass in her pocket. "Root beer must be popular around here."

I waved Baby's check at her, and she gave me a hug. "Good for you, sweetheart," she said. "I knew something positive would happen today. It was in the horoscope."

Janelle didn't believe in horoscopes and neither did I, but we had begun following the one that came out in the local weekly. It was unusually specific and insistent; sometimes it seemed to be directed at particular individuals. I had read mine that morning: "How big can you dream? How much can you accept? Love and money will come your way when you conquer your fears. Quit making excuses!" We occasionally spotted the astrologer driving around town in her van, which had the All-Seeing Eye of Providence painted on the side. "I guess I should pay more attention," I said.

"Word," said Janelle. "I had a lucky day too."

"New client?" I asked, remembering the horoscope's prediction of money.

"Better," she said. "I went for a mammogram this morning. At the clinic in town."

I gasped. "I'm so sorry, Janelle. I forgot all about it." As I had been flirting with Baby on the phone, Janelle had been stripping down to her underwear and putting on a hospital johnny. *Opening in the front, please.*

"It's okay," she said. To my relief, she seemed genuinely calm. "It's still clear."

She ran out to buy a bottle of wine to celebrate our various accomplishments—"A good bottle," she admonished me, and I didn't ask her what it cost—and after dinner we had a hilarious time rolling around in bed, with me feeling unusually sensitive all over my body. She kept me away from her breasts. "Sore," she said. Just as we were nodding off, she murmured in my ear, "Love you—baby."

Uh-oh, I remembered. But I woke the next morning feeling simply grateful for the sun shining through the window and the pigeons hooting and Janelle beside me, sleeping on her back with her arms thrown over her head, in the pose, if she had been upright, of someone reacting to a nice surprise, so I woke her by sucking on her nipples and for a change she liked it, and we both had a couple of orgasms before breakfast. Then she left for the office, and I sat down at the work table I had set up in our little spare room, but instead of getting started on Baby's jewelry order, I became lost in thoughts of Baby herself.

And of Janelle. When I had first started dating her, Roger had asked me out for coffee, saying he wanted to get to know me. Actually, he wanted to warn me. "Nora," he had said, "you seem like a good person, and I can tell I'm going to like you. But *do not fuck this up.*" That was what I reminded myself of now—because I could see I was on the verge of getting myself into just the sort of trouble I had told Baby I wasn't looking for. I had been in triangles before—what lesbian hasn't?—and I thought I knew better than to carpe diem. As you grabbed for that shiny new thing, you were likely to lose both it and the one you already had. I had become older, wiser, weightier. Like a truck, I required more room to clear the corners, I thought.

Yet, must that require avoiding new acquaintances and experiences? I asked myself. And if so, why had we bothered moving? With such rationalizations, I picked up the phone and hit redial. "Wanna go swimming?" I asked my new friend. If that's what she was.

"It's December."

"I'm aware of that," I said. "I'm going to go every month."

"Ah, one of those," said Baby. "You're on."

Pink Towel

Baby cheated. She showed up wearing a wet suit. Gorgeous, it made no secret of her belly and butt.

The day was sunny and cloudless, with a hard, steady wind. Even at Herring Cove Beach, which is on the bay, so somewhat sheltered—on the clearest days you could see all the way to Plymouth, and a tower belonging to the nuclear power plant, or maybe it was Boston, and a harmless skyscraper, depending on whom you asked—there were whitecaps and rolling waves breaking onto the shore with a clatter of pebbles. The gulls were swinging wildly back and forth, and farther out you could see the telltale splashes of a flock of gannets dive-bombing mackerel. Sitting in the car with the heater blasting, I had been trying to see the scene as a late August afternoon with the wind kicking up. But the cold outside was palpable.

I stuck my head out the window. "No fair," I yelled to Baby.

She came over and leaned on my car for balance while she yanked off her boots. "What?" she said, attempting to tuck all her hair into an old-fashioned rubber bathing cap decorated with yellow daisies.

I jumped out of the car and stripped down to my speedo. "I have to do this fast, or I won't go through with it," I said and took off down the beach. My extremities must have frozen instantly, because I couldn't feel the rocks underfoot. Everyone complains about them; some have paranoid theories: "Of course the *gay* beach is the one with the rocks. You don't see any rocks at Race Point." I hoped Baby was following behind me, but I didn't turn around to look. Without stopping, I flung myself into the sea.

Rush of green bubbles. White foam. Salt taste. Crash up from

23

freezing water into freezing air. Breathe in. Breathe out. *Whah!* Flail to shore. Run back over pebbles.

Baby was standing next to my car holding open a big pink towel. "That was fast," she said, enfolding me in the towel and vigorously rubbing my arms and back to warm me. After a moment, I took it from her to dry my hair.

When I looked up, she was strolling down to the water. She did a little knee bend, a leap up on the rebound, and dove into a wave. Her yellow head popped up in the trough, and she stroked leisurely back and forth along the shoreline a few times. I watched her, and the gulls and the gannets. How did they stand it? Finally she emerged and picked her way up the beach to the car. "Refreshing!" she said.

Even back in my dry clothes, I couldn't stop shivering. "I guess this isn't for me," I admitted.

"You don't have hypothermia if you're still shivering. You'll get used to it. Let's go for coffee; it'll warm you up."

"You're wearing a wet suit, red boots, and a flowered bathing cap," I pointed out.

"Keeping your head warm is the key. And this is P-town, my dear. No one will look twice. But if you don't feel comfortable—"

"It's not that," I said. "I'm freezing. I need to put on a sweatshirt and a pair of warm socks. And Janelle will wonder what happened to me."

"Cold feet and a guilty conscience," said Baby. "I must be getting somewhere."

"I have work to do," I insisted. "For you, your shop." I turned the key in the ignition.

"Work it good, then," said Baby.

When I looked in the rearview mirror, she was wiggling her fingers good-bye. She saw me noticing and blew me a kiss. Trouble indeed. On the way home, I kept thinking about that towel, and what might have happened if it hadn't come between Baby's hands and my skin.

As I said, in Provincetown I became a cad.

My Heart

I thought maybe a different perspective would help, and I called Roger. "I'm doing what you told me not to, Roger. I'm fucking up. Save me from myself!" He still lived in the city, running the old rat race. We had begged him to come to Provincetown with us when we decided to move, but although we were serious, he never seriously considered it. People move with their lovers, but not with their friends, not even with those they consider their "gay family," as Roger and Janelle and I had toasted each other on many occasions.

Roger taught third grade, and every afternoon on his way home, he stopped at the gym and worked out for an hour and a half. We had never known him to have a steady boyfriend, and although he would moan about it sometimes, he was actually quite pleased with his life. He had lots of sex, lots of friends, his apartment was pristine, and if he wanted to walk out of a movie, he didn't have to explain himself to anyone.

"I haven't heard from you in weeks," said Roger. "Now you call. Something's up. But do I care?"

"It hasn't been weeks; it's been days," I said.

"Weeks, days," said Roger. "Einstein said time is subjective."

"Oh, he did not!" I said. "And if he did, he meant the cosmos, not Brooklyn."

"Perhaps," said Roger. "I was out late last night with Blaze, and then this afternoon my charges were blessed with such a surfeit of energy—"

"Wait a minute," I said. "Blaze? Isn't that a name for a horse?"

"An animal of some sort," Roger agreed. "Finally I had the little angels run a race around the schoolyard, and the girls' team won, which

25

caused a predictable uproar. I allowed a do-over, and of course the girls won again. I'm fried. How is the beautiful and charming Janelle?"

"That's why I called," I said. "You've got to help me. I've been flirting. We went swimming, and she rubbed me down with her towel."

Roger sighed. "My dear," he said. "You are a fool. And I would hate to have to give you up."

"How can you say that so casually?" I gasped.

"Janelle wouldn't stand for it," he said. "I was her friend first."

"But I'm not leaving her!" I insisted. "I don't want to leave her! I'm thinking brief affair."

"I sympathize," said Roger. "But you *lesbianas* are so strange about these things."

"What if she never finds out?" I asked. I had been giving a lot of thought to logistics. Janelle worked predictable hours in her office. I stayed home, responsible for nothing much but dinner and Baby's jewelry order. Which I would of course have to consult with her about.

"In that *village* you're living in? Are you tripping? Talk about a fuckup waiting to happen," said Roger. "Don't break my girlfriend's heart. Especially after everything she's been through."

"What about *my* heart?" I decided to lay on him all the rationalizations I had come up with, to see how he took them. "It would just be an interlude. I've been through a lot too. Look how depressed I was. Janelle's not easy."

"As I'm well aware," said Roger. "Well aware. But I mean what I said. And by the way, I don't think that's called your *heart*. At least, that's not what we learned in biology class. Get a grip, girl!"

That was unhelpful, I thought as I put down the phone. I was trying to figure out who else I could call but realized absolutely no one was going to tell me what I wanted to hear; I wouldn't even tell it to myself.

Asparagus

Annoyingly, Roger was right. Of course it wasn't my heart that was throbbing, and it wasn't love that I was looking for. I had that, and I thought I knew enough to hang onto it. All I wanted was a short shock, a jolt, a sizzle. A little thrill.

I was arranging and rearranging beads and pieces of beach glass into pleasing shape and color combinations on my work table when the phone rang. Hoping it was Roger, apologizing, or some nicer, more sympathetic friend, or at least a telemarketer I could yell at, I grabbed it.

"How about coffee today?" asked Baby. "I'm wearing street clothes, and it's pretty warm out."

"Um . . . um," I said. I had no excuse. Or didn't want one. "Come over here. I do great work with a French press."

"A French what?" said Baby. "I'll be right there."

I put down the phone, and it immediately started ringing again. *Maybe she's canceling*, I thought dejectedly. *Maybe she's canceling*, I thought hopefully.

"I'm going to swing by the Stop & Shop," said Janelle. "Want anything?"

"How about a bunch of asparagus?" I said, naming an impossible vegetable. Janelle enjoyed the occasional time-consuming grocery hunt. "We haven't had that in a while."

"Because it's almost winter, honey child," she pointed out.

"You can do it," I said. "See if they have local, not those dried-up sticks from South Africa."

It's amazing how fast a life can change. One day, I was half of a peaceful, loving couple; the next, apparently, a libido-driven maniac. I

almost called Baby back to cancel. Then I rationalized. Surely Janelle and
I had gone way beyond patriarchal notions of ownership and jealousy.
We enjoyed a deep and, we believed, abiding love, so much so that in all
our years together, we had never actually sat down and had the Talk:
open or closed; don't-ask-don't-tell or tell-all; exceptions such as professional conferences, high school reunions, encounters outside of a two-
hundred-mile radius. For a lot of people, geography made a difference.
I had a friend—she admitted to certain issues with intimacy—who had
arrived at an understanding with an ornithologist who spent six months
of each year in Antarctica. "Every pot has its cover," my grandmother
would have said, in the unlikely circumstance that she had been inspired
to comment on lesbian fidelity.

I heard a *tak-tok-tak-tok* coming down the sidewalk and went to
look out the front door. Baby smiled and wiggled her fingers hello. "I
have to tell you something," she called.

"You're married," I said. Of course, I realized. The whole exciting
mess had been a big delusion on my part.

"Don't be silly," she said. "I've had too much coffee already today.
If I have any more I'll get a headache."

"Tea?" I offered.

"Actually, just water would be fine."

"Water?" I said. No one drank Provincetown water. It caused terrible
stomach cramps. Only the tourists asked for ice in their drinks. Some
year-rounders also mistrusted the jugs of house brand from the Stop &
Shop. There was a rumor that the night manager filled them from a secret tap at the back of the parking lot.

"You have some Poland Spring in the fridge, don't you?"

"I've learned that much," I said as she entered my home and fell into
my arms. I extricated myself to shut the door behind her, then took her
hand and led her into my studio. It was a tiny room, under the eaves, not
constructed to accommodate two full-grown, active adults, careening
and rolling around it, banging into my work table, scattering beads and
beach glass all over ourselves. At one point, with Baby kneeling above

me, I held her breasts in my hands, then pressed them together to suck both nipples at once—a trick I hadn't been allowed to practice in a while. She moaned and arched her back and then collapsed on top of me, trapping my arm between us, but I was able to work my hand down her belly and slide a finger around her clitoris.

Oh," she gasped. "Like that. Just like that. Oh, good girl." We rocked together, Baby periodically shuddering and murmuring in my ear, "That. Oh, that," until finally she sighed deeply and lay still.

Then she touched me, and it was—I don't know—like the ceiling fell in. I had never heard of lesbian premature ejaculation, but that first time with Baby, *wham*. I came instantly and hard. I may have momentarily lost consciousness. I took her hand. "No more," I said.

Baby didn't seem disconcerted. We lay still for a while, then she sat up, shook out her hair, and said, "My, my, Nora Griffin. You surely are something special." She leaned over and gave me a final smooch. "Oof. My back. Stay right there, sweet thing. I'll just wash up and let myself out."

I let her go. I lay on the floor of my studio in a stunned condition, while my new paramour *tak-tok-tak-tok*-ed out the front door and down the street.

Once she left, the floor started to feel uncomfortable, but I considered staying there and allowing myself to fall into a deep sleep—only because I didn't want to analyze what had just happened, or anticipate what might happen next. No, not *what had just happened*—I forced myself to think the words: Sex. With Baby. It was inconceivable, even as the facts proved otherwise. The disarranged furniture. The beads on the floor. I hadn't had sex with anyone but Janelle for a decade, and I swore to my good angel that it would never happen again.

Except maybe, whispered the other angel.

I sat up quickly, brushed a few pieces of beach glass off my shirt, and went into the kitchen to find a glass of water and the broom. That's when Janelle came home.

"Oh. Hi. Hi there!" I said.

"Why are you looking at me funny?" asked Janelle. "And why are you talking so weird? Are you high?"

"Of course I'm not high. And I'm not looking at you funny. I'm just looking. You walked into the room."

She noticed the broom in my hands. I rarely did nonemergency cleaning, and she followed me into the studio, where I madly started sweeping. "Wow, what happened in here?" she said. "You're a mess, sweetheart. Your shirt's buttoned wrong. Come here and let me fix you."

I had no choice. I put down the broom and walked over to her, and she put a finger under my chin and lifted my face to hers. I tried and tried, but I couldn't meet her eyes. And as she looked at me, her expression changed from concern to comprehension.

"You have that look on your face. I'd know it anywhere," she said slowly. "I can't believe this is happening."

"Janelle—" I said stupidly.

"Don't talk to me," she said. "You have purple lipstick on your collar! I thought that was just a dumb song."

"I love you, Janelle," I whispered.

"Liar!" Janelle exclaimed. "I told you, don't talk to me. Don't say my name! Just get out of my sight! Get out of my house! This is my house!"

"But—" I attempted. Although I had nothing to say for myself.

"How could you do this?" she cried. "Now, of all times! Like I don't have enough to deal with!" She grabbed me, and with one hand around my bicep and the other on my back, she pushed me down the hall and out the front door. "Get! Out! Now!" she yelled. "I thought I could count on you. You're nothing to me anymore! Nothing!" She slammed the door after me. At certain bad moments, I can still feel the imprint of her palm between my shoulder blades.

There I was, standing on Commercial Street, with nothing but the clothes on my back. I went back and tried the door, but she had locked it. Unfair, I thought. She hadn't even bothered to ask for my side of the story—whatever that was. I could have concocted something if she had given me a chance. Pounding on the door, I shouted, "Hey, Janelle, come on, it's freezing out! This is my place too! What am I supposed to do?" In a minute the neighbors would be peeking out their windows to see what the commotion was about. Some dykes. At it, as usual. "I'm sorry!" I offered pathetically.

She opened the door a crack, with the chain across it. I didn't know our door even had a chain—wasn't that one of the reasons we had moved from Brooklyn, to do away with locks and chains? "Betrayer! Figure it out yourself for once," she yelled. "You are *disgusting*. And this is not your home anymore. You violated it." From behind the door, she pushed out my down jacket, my wallet, and a plastic grocery sack. "I mean it, Nora, I never want to see you again. You made your choice." She closed the door, and I heard the lock turn. I put on my jacket, stuck the wallet in my pocket, and looked in the sack. Asparagus.

The Universe Comes
to a Halt but Quickly
Starts Up Again

I had no idea what to do, where to go, whom to call. Baby was out of the question—going to her would confirm every bad thing Janelle suspected me of, and anyway, the thought of Baby made me feel, just at that moment, bruised. Roger had already made clear his opinion of my escapade. In a state of shock, I wandered in circles in front of my former home. I thought Janelle might see my distress, but when I looked up at the windows, the curtains were closed. She would never relent. I didn't even think she should relent. I was scum. Vile scum.

I wandered off, destination-less, making an anxious mental list of the people I had met so far in Provincetown: The Jamaican cashiers in the Stop & Shop. The librarian—she had checked out books for me several times, and I had seen her once in the post office, but she was always silent, as befits a librarian, and since we had never exchanged a word, maybe she didn't count. I had had an interesting conversation with the Unitarian minister when I had signed up for the craft fair—she volunteered on a team that rescued stranded dolphins in the spring and feral cats in the fall—and I had felt an instant bond with the woman who had cut my hair, who was also a newcomer to town, although she had come all the way from Moldova, while I had only traveled up the Northeast Corridor. But I realized I hadn't learned anyone's address, so I couldn't suddenly turn up to crash on her couch, even if I had had the nerve to.

I opened the bag and tried a stalk of asparagus—not great. Janelle had been less of a head-turning success than usual. But tears welled up in my eyes at the thought of her trying so hard because of my supposed whim, hunting through the vegetable counters in every understocked corner store between Provincetown and Wellfleet as Baby and I frolicked. How could I have done such a thing? When I came to a trash barrel, I crumpled up the bag and threw it in. I found a tissue at the bottom of my jacket pocket, blew my nose, and threw the tissue in too. Then I just stood there, next to the trash barrel. I couldn't think of a reason to move. My life force, or whatever it is that keeps us humans running around all day, had evaporated.

Miss Ruby

Hey, girlie!" A large woman on one of those riding scooters they advertise on cable TV had come to a stop, too, in the middle of the street. I stared at her. *Maybe it was happening to everyone.* Dressed in gray sweats, with gray hair decimated by alopecia, the woman was remarkably shapeless and colorless. Her scooter, though, was candy-apple red, and she had decorated the basket in the front with plastic roses. "Give us a push? I think the motor's busted."

Dutifully, I went over and pushed her to a curb cut and up onto the sidewalk. It was surprisingly difficult to get the contraption moving without its motor.

"Thanks." She held out her hand. "Miss Ruby."

I shook her hand. "Nora Griffin," I said. "What are you going to do? Is there some kind of Triple A for these things?"

"I don't think so," she said. "I've never had a problem with it before."

"I left without my phone," I said. "Or I could call someone for you."

"I don't have one either," she said. "Don't trust 'em." She reached into the basket and pulled out a large, trapezoidal purse, the kind that closes with two gold beads and is full of used tissues, and arranged the handles over her shoulder. "My place is up the street. I think we can make it."

She slid off the seat, grabbed my arm, and clung to me like the Old Man of the Sea. Steering me around the corner, she said to herself, "Shouldn't have worn house slippers."

"Don't try to talk," I said. We had progressed only about half a block, but she was breathing heavily.

"Stop a minute," she panted. "Coming to the hard part."

34

Provincetown is built on dunes; everything slopes up from Commercial Street and the harbor. As we rested, a small white pickup pulled up to us, honking. "Scooter break down again, Rube?" the driver called out the window.

"Ignore her," said Miss Ruby. She pulled on my sleeve, and we began stumbling up the street again. "My place," she wheezed. "Over there."

She took a hand off my shoulder to wave in the direction of a little cottage. Many of the larger houses had one or two of these built in the yard, to cram a few summer visitors into during the season. This one had quaint weathered shingles, like a lot of P-town structures, but looking closer, you could see that many were missing, and the trim had not been painted in so long that like the shingles it was gray, with a few cracked ribbons of white still clinging to the wood. A patch of lawn held a No Vacancy sign. At the door, Miss Ruby scrabbled around in her purse for her key but came up empty-handed.

"Pants pocket?" I suggested.

Too winded to talk, she held up her index finger, felt around her waistband, and produced a key. The door opened into a living room. We had barely gotten ourselves inside when what seemed like a million cats surrounded us and began rubbing our legs. Miss Ruby reached down to pet a few and made kissy faces at the rest as she tottered over to an enormous recliner that was the room's centerpiece and fell into it, trying to catch her breath. Noticing that I was still standing in the doorway, surrounded and trying not to step on any tails, she shouted hoarsely at me, "For goddess's sake, girl! Don't let 'em out!" Two or three startled cats streaked away before I could slam the door, but Miss Ruby didn't seem to notice. "Water," she panted, pointing to the kitchen.

I went in, found a glass, and without thinking turned on the faucet.

"Are you trying to kill me?" Miss Ruby called. "Get it from the refrigerator!"

"Sorry." I did as she demanded, and back in the living room, I handed her the glass.

On a side table next to her chair was an array of pill bottles, jars, and inhalers of various colors and shapes, a box of tissues, a phone, the television clicker, a stack of crossword puzzle books, and a pile of dirty dishes. She popped a couple of pills, puffed on one of the inhalers, and produced a pack of Marlboros from her purse. Lighting up, she blew a couple of smoke rings in my direction. "Take a load off," she offered, gesturing at an armchair next to hers. "What a day!"

I couldn't stop myself. "That can't be good for you," I said, sitting down.

"You believe every damn thing they stick on the side of a package?" She pointed the clicker at the television and turned to a channel that was showing what looked like a video of the craft fair. The camera panned the hall, then zoomed dizzily in and out to show quick close-ups of the tables. I could see the mistake I had made putting out the books next to my quite nice jewelry; they lowered the tone of the whole setup. Settling in with a whining Siamese in her lap, Miss Ruby looked at me expectantly. "So, Nora Griffin. What's your story?"

"It's hard to say." I couldn't seem to grasp how I had ended up choking on cat hair and cigarette smoke in Miss Ruby's living room, and when I tried to organize my thoughts about the past couple of weeks, all I saw was a blur. A few colors stood out: A gift of amber beach glass. A pink towel. "There was Baby and, you know—"

"Ha! Ha!" coughed Miss Ruby. "Good old Baby!"

"—Janelle kicked me out. But maybe she didn't mean permanently. She's the kind of person who gets mad, but then it blows over." Actually, Janelle had never exhibited this sort of behavior, and neither had anyone else I had ever known, but I had heard of it. Lesbians, in my experience, were more likely to stew over things for years, then let it all out in a big awful scene from which there was no return. "Maybe I should try going back."

Miss Ruby stubbed out her cigarette. "You can't go home again," she said, nodding at her wisdom. "It's a good thing I picked you up; you seem like you could use a helping hand. Take the spare room. The

No Vacancy sign is just for strangers. Sheets and towels are in the bureau. You'll have to make the bed yourself; I can't do all that bending anymore." A ten-year-old in a crooked tutu twirled across the TV screen, catching her attention. "Hey, that's little Danny Pereira! Looking good, don't you think? Graceful."

Miss Ruby spent her nights—and most days, now that her scooter was in the shop—in her chair, smoking, napping, and hacking up her lungs, the TV constantly muttering in the background. Sometimes she muttered back. "Cheers me up," she said. "Hope it doesn't bother you."

Maybe that first night at Miss Ruby's wasn't the worst of my life, but I can't think of another. Every time I started to doze off, the TV or Miss Ruby's coughing seemed to reach a crescendo, or I had a sneezing fit or an unscratchable itch in the middle of my back. My attempts to realistically assess my situation degenerated into insomniac raving. Words stuck in my head, the way songs sometimes did: *Asparagus*, for hours. *Beach glass*. Toward morning, *boobs*—a word I don't even like. Janelle's breasts—well, that was one story. And Baby's were exemplars of their kind, big and soft and beautiful. If only I hadn't been sweeping. If only I had been working, Janelle might not have noticed. But no, I had to sweep. Sweep, sweep, sweep.

I felt grateful to Miss Ruby for taking me in off the street, literally, and I felt sorry for her for being so sick and weak, but when the sky outside began to brighten, and the mourning doves started up with their endless chanting—in exactly the rhythm of the death march—and the TV was still yammering, and I still hadn't fallen asleep, I realized her environment was simply intolerable. And yet I didn't see a way out. There probably was one, and if, I berated myself, instead of lying on Miss Ruby's lumpy cot, I would just stand up, and let the night's thoughts sift out of my head and float meaninglessly to the floor with the rest of the dust, I could probably find it. I rolled over and buried my head in the pillow. Then I couldn't breathe.

Bitches

I bought a package of underpants, some socks, and a toothbrush at the hardware store, which carried a surprising assortment of daily necessities, but I knew that was only a temporary solution. It took me a week to work up the courage to call Janelle, and she reluctantly agreed to allow me into the house. Once. She didn't ask where I was staying, or anything else. "And don't bring that bitch around here," she said.

"Actually, if you must know, I haven't seen her since—"

"Please don't tell me about your relationship problems."

I had been avoiding Baby, although not because I didn't want to see her. I longed to, but I was confused. My head was constantly stuffed and my nose running, and my eyes were so swollen I couldn't see straight—or maybe I was starting to hallucinate from lack of sleep. Miss Ruby kept me remarkably busy, picking up her prescriptions, running all over town to find bargains on cigarettes and over to the shopping plaza when she had a yen for a beer or a pint of Häagen-Dazs. She didn't seem to eat much real food, and I had started to get out of the habit myself. She hadn't found anyone to fix her scooter, so she really was stuck, and I felt obliged to help her, since she didn't seem to have anyone else to do it. Also, she hadn't asked me to pay for the room.

"I won't be around, so I'm trusting you on this," said Janelle. "Although I don't know why. Roger says I was naïve all along."

"Then he's a bitch too," I said. "That is totally untrue."

"But how can I believe you?" asked Janelle.

For a moment she sounded less angry than sad, and I felt awash in guilt—almost literally, as though she had dumped a bucket of freezing liquid guilt over my head.

On moving day, the Unitarian minister helped me pack and carry boxes out to her van. She had offered to store my stuff in the church. "It's against the rules, but should we be bound by irrational regulations?" she mused. "An interesting moral question."

Sorting through my art supplies, I realized that Janelle had repossessed all the beach glass she had found for me. "Shit!" I burst out. "What next? That was going to be my livelihood! Fuck!" I remembered the minister. "Sorry, Reverend Patsy."

"No problem," she said, staring at me intently, which I thought was odd until I realized she was trying to convey sympathy. She had a gray, do-it-yourself, bowl haircut, aviator glasses that were so out of style I kept wondering where she had found them, and an oversized nose. Something about her, although I couldn't figure out exactly what, screamed religious—nun, pastor. She could even have been a rabbi, except for the collar, which she seemed to enjoy wearing in all circumstances— like now, hauling boxes back and forth. I could just see her dressed for dolphin rescue, in a baggy tank suit and the collar. "I'm sorry you're experiencing this difficult time," she said.

"Miss Ruby says you can't go home again," I said.

She nodded and stared at me some more.

"Of course, Janelle says that too," I added.

I didn't have that much stuff, relatively, but I think it was more than Reverend Patsy had anticipated. We arranged the boxes around her office to create a path to her desk, and I promised her I would move them out really soon, although I felt unhappy about that, since I had no foreseeable way to actually come through. "No problem," she repeated, but less forcefully. "If anyone wants pastoral counseling they'll have their choice of places to sit." She was being so nice to me, and I didn't even belong to her church—I decided to go to a Sunday service sometime, although I had never had any particular religious preference. It would be a new experience. Then I remembered I had had enough of new experiences.

Removing the last of my things from what I guess had been Janelle's house all along made me feel unmoored and weightless, if not totally hysterical. "Can I use your phone?" I asked Reverend Patsy.

Baby picked up right away. "Nora, sweetie!" she cried out. "I've been so worried! There's something wrong with your phone. Every time I try to call you, it seems like it answers, but then there's just a click. I didn't know what happened to you! I thought maybe you had gone back to Brooklyn."

"Just to Miss Ruby's," I said. "She found me on the street after Janelle threw me out."

"Threw you out!" said Baby. "Get over here right now and tell me what happened."

"I'm a wreck," I said.

"Well, of course," said Baby. "Who wouldn't be, after all that, and Miss Ruby."

"She keeps the TV on all the time!" I said. "She has a thousand cats!"

When I arrived, Baby turned the sign on her shop door from "open" to "closed." She lived in a studio in the back, which sounds modest, but it was literally on the beach, with a grand window onto the harbor.

"It's amazing during a storm," she said. "With the birds blowing around and the waves crashing over the deck, you would think you're on the *Titanic*."

"I have to tell you something," I said. "It's going to be a while before I can manufacture those earrings for your store. Janelle took back all my beach glass. The stuff's hard to find; she was really good at it."

"We'll figure that out later," said Baby, taking me into her arms.

"All I've done is think of you," I sighed.

"But not really," she murmured, kissing a particularly lovely spot on my neck and causing an electric current to zing through me and out my toes. "When there's so much else going on."

"Oh, yes," I said. "Yes." I may have sounded a little Molly Bloomish right then, but what I had told her was true. She had hovered over all of it—losing Janelle, getting found by Miss Ruby, her cats, my boxes. And you might think that in such a crisis—set off, after all, when Baby had *tak-tok-tak-tok*-ed into my life—I would have been distracted and anxious, even regretful, and unresponsive to her touch. But that's not how it was. Instead, I snapped to attention, completely and utterly and helplessly present to Baby.

The Green Teddy

After we showered and dressed, Baby turned the shop sign from "closed" back to "open," and we sat behind the counter together and talked about what to do. It felt oddly peaceful and even intimate, in the off-season lull. In the bleak depths of December, most of the traffic on Commercial Street was made up of trucks full of construction materials, and bursts from jack hammers and chainsaws periodically drowned out the melancholy hooting of the pigeons and the foghorns.

The guys in their big muddy boots and fluorescent vests mostly weren't interested in jewelry and crafts, so Baby and I, like the other shopkeepers, weren't often interrupted by customers. In fact, one had started to use the slow afternoons for phone sessions with her psychoanalyst, until she realized that word had gotten around, and everyone in town was trying to interpret her dreams. Others took advantage of the time to slap additions onto their houses, which the Board of Selectmen would then demand they remove, saying they ruined the historical character of the town. The owners would refuse, and everyone would have a good time writing letters to the local paper and filing lawsuits, until the additions had been up so long they could be grandfathered in.

The selectmen were perpetually, hopelessly, campaigning against P-town's tackiness; one summer, knowing they would never make any headway against drag queens like Cher, standing elegantly on her electric skateboard and blowing kisses to the summer crowds, they had instead banned the Lobster Man, a loudmouth in a red plush suit who had handed out flyers for a local restaurant. He had been genuinely annoying, so there wasn't much of a fuss—but then they banned the kid who sold pink-frosted cupcakes from a card table on a corner after the bars let out. They claimed that he should have applied for a catering license. The drag queens, who loved the cupcakes, came to his defense and took up a collection, which was so successful he was able to open a bakery.

"I wish I could afford to hire you in the shop," said Baby. "You need a job."

"A different place to live, too," I said gloomily.

"Can you pull espresso?" asked Baby.

"Aren't I a little old for that?" I said. "Baby, you might not realize it but back in Brooklyn I was teaching, I'd made a few sales, an agent was interested in me, and I was on my way to a solo show. I was developing an actual career."

"Okay, but I have a feeling we're not in Brooklyn anymore, Toto, darling."

I remembered the scene in the movie where Dorothy and her friends go to that spa in Oz city. "You mean it's all service jobs."

"Come with me," said Baby, jumping up. She was not one to sit around when she might be taking action, and I rushed after her. When we arrived at a busy coffee shop in one of those tiny house-like structures that Provincetown seems to specialize in, she pointed triumphantly at a sign on the door. "Check it out. I thought I remembered it."

"'Use other door'?" I read, to tease her. But I really wasn't so happy about where this was going.

"You are a nut," she said, giving me a playful kiss. I returned it, and we scuffled enjoyably for a moment in the entryway. "The other sign!"

"'Experienced help wanted,'" I said. "But I don't have experience."

"Jeez, Nora, how hard could it be?" she said.

"Hey, lesbians—keep it clean over there!" someone boomed at us.

"Hey, Bob!" Baby greeted him. Turning back to me, she explained, "He's the one you have to talk to." Bob had the height and build of a linebacker, and a shaved head—although unfortunately he wasn't one of those people with a beautiful round skull to show off; his was lumpy, more like Nikita Khrushchev's, ears and all. He was wearing a leather vest

and big black boots, an outfit that I later discovered he wore year-round—
with jeans and a T-shirt under the vest in the winter; running shorts and
nothing under the vest but his hirsute chest and back in the summer.
He would have terrified me if he hadn't also sported, tucked into his
vest pocket, a small, colorful stuffed bear—Green Teddy, GT for short,
for whom the coffee shop was named. "His friends call him Babs," said
Baby. "Some night we'll go catch his drag act at the Crown and Anchor."

"Baby!" he called again. "I love you! Get over here!" Bob/Babs was a
true washashore. The story was that he had been a top executive—how
high up depended on who was telling it—at a transnational corporation
that hawked various climate-killing widgets, dressing every day in one
from his wardrobe of suits custom made for his height and girth. At a
certain point, it had all crashed. Some of those whispering on the Green
Teddy patio claimed he had actually done time, but most disputed this.
No one does time for corporate busts, they pointed out—it wasn't like
he had just kited a few checks—and anyway, Bob never seemed hardened
or depressed. He did have a lot of tattoos, but they weren't the jailhouse
kind. In P-town he did yoga, he meditated, and he said he was practicing
gratefulness. A perfectionist, he told me I would need months of training
before I would develop the necessary skills to use his imported Italian
espresso machine, but he hired me anyway, to sweep the patio and ring
up the customers. We shook hands on the deal.

"But why so formal?" he said. "We're friends now!" He held out his
arms. "Hugs, hugs!" he insisted, enfolding me.

Baby turned away from a conversation she had been having with
one of the baristas, a muscled Valkyrie with two long, blonde braids
wrapped in a crown around her head and a Polynesian armband tattoo
that would grow more elaborate every week. "See," Baby told me. "Everything's going to be fine."

"Who was that?" I asked.

"Who was who?" said Baby. I pointed at the barista. "Brunhilde? I
call her Broony. Come on, let's go back to my place and make dinner."

So we did. We made dinner, we made love, and the next morning, I walked back to Miss Ruby's, somewhat dazed from all our activity, somewhat ecstatic, somewhat depressed, somewhat employed. A frigid, salty fog was rolling around the streets, coalescing periodically into snow flurries, the season's first, and I realized I had never before seen snow on a beach. Out on the bay, the moored boats disappeared into the mist.

And I was adrift, I knew, like a dinghy in the fog.

The White Pickup Truck

When I got back to Miss Ruby's, the white pickup truck was parked outside. In the living room, sitting in what I had begun to think of as my chair, was a short, wiry butch of about Miss Ruby's age, wearing a camouflage-patterned T-shirt and khaki work pants. Her wavy gray hair was squashed down on top from a severe case of hat-head clearly caused by the trucker's cap she held in her lap. The place seemed different, and I realized the shades were up. I hadn't noticed before that the room had so many windows. The TV was off, and the cats were trying to hide in a pile in the corner. "What the hell's been going on here?" she demanded.

"Tony," explained Miss Ruby, waving at her visitor. "Nora."

"She's smoking like a chimney, she hasn't gone out of the house in a week, the scooter's chained to a parking meter down on Commercial, the freezer's full of ice cream, and the whole damn place smells like beer and cat pee, *Norma*." Tony sneered the name like it was a synonym for "cat pee." It wasn't one of my favorites either.

"Nora," I corrected her. "This is Miss Ruby's home. I didn't think it was my place to start telling her how to live."

"Yeah, well, I call that enabling," said Tony.

"She's twelve step," Miss Ruby whispered to me.

"Twelve step nothing," Tony said loudly. "I call it irresponsible." She turned to me. "She's done this before. She asks some sweet little Girl Scout to help her cross the street or something, and *bam*! Next thing you know, the rescue squad is all over the place and she ends up in that lousy Cape Cod Hospital on oxygen. *Norma*."

"But *she's* helping *me*," I said.

46

"Well. That's a new one," said Tony. "Get this place in order. I'll go down and fix the scooter." She stomped out the door.

Miss Ruby groaned. "She doesn't know a damn thing about motors; she just likes having an excuse to wear her tool belt. The mechanic will charge me twice as much after she gets done with it."

"She's right though," I said.

"Tony?" said Miss Ruby, pointing the clicker at the TV. "She's always right."

Miss Ruby's cottage was so small that dusting and vacuuming weren't really much of a chore, and I wondered guiltily why I hadn't cleaned as soon as I arrived. Exposed to light and cleared of hairballs, the place felt almost wholesome. If I took pills for the cat hair and got a supply of ear plugs for the TV, I realized, it would be close to livable.

Miss Ruby beckoned to the cats, and several jumped into her lap. She lit a cigarette. "I suppose you want me to cut down on these things, too," she said.

"Quit, actually," I said. "If I'm going to stay. You'll feel a lot better when you can breathe, Miss Ruby."

"And we were having such fun," she sighed.

Pulling Espresso

The Green Teddy gig was not an immediate success. On my first day, Bob had just introduced me to my coworkers and was teaching me how to work the cash register when Janelle and Roger walked in. Although she was an early riser, he wasn't, at least not on weekends. He prided himself, though, on being a superpolite and self-effacing guest, so he must have been trying to accommodate her schedule. That would end, I suspected, after he had spent a late night or two of cooking elegant dinners, failing to persuade Janelle to go out dancing with him afterward, and then, when the bars closed, trying to scare up some off-season action at the Dick Dock.

"School vacation?" I asked Roger. I hoped that if I could get him to talk to me, maybe Janelle would too.

The two of them stared at me wordlessly, turned around, and stomped out. I felt slapped.

"Intense," said Bob. "Do you often have that effect on people?"

"Just them." I had never been cut so decisively before. A myriad of experiences in those weeks had confronted me with just how thoroughly I had *fucked up*—but it was only after that encounter with Janelle and Roger that I truly understood my life would never be the same.

"Well, don't scare away any more of my customers." He laughed, oblivious or perhaps entertained by my problems. I hoped I had accumulated more acquaintances, who would take my side, than Janelle had. A drawback of small-town life was becoming clear to me: word got around.

"Okay, guys, here goes!" said Bob, clapping his hands. I looked up to find that a long queue had materialized, winding around the little store, out the door to the patio, and down the front stoop. "This is our morning rush, Nora," he explained. "José will be here in a second; he's a regular. He'll want to hang out and gossip for twenty minutes while you ring people up, so I hope you got the hang of the register. He takes an extra-large red-eye, but don't charge him for the shot today. I like to comp him every once in a while."

"Got it, boss," I said, feeling bewildered. Then I didn't have time to feel anything. A shift at the Green Teddy was like stepping off the platform onto the playground slide: the morning rush zoomed past and into the afternoon rush, and at the end I landed with a bump onto the patio, a bit vertiginous, but on my feet.

"That wasn't too bad, was it?" said Baby. She had arrived just as promised to pick me up after my inaugural shift, a treat to get me through my first day.

"It'll cover the rent, I guess," I said. "Miss Ruby says she'll quit smoking if I pay her." At Tony's direction, we had worked out an agreement. Miss Ruby would do the shopping on her scooter, and I would cook and clean the litterboxes. Tony would make frequent, unannounced visits to make sure we weren't slacking off. Although Miss Ruby grumbled, I could tell that underneath, she enjoyed having Tony's attention, while Tony, for her part, seemed gleeful about having us to instruct and mold.

"So you have an okay place to stay," said Baby. She had been chatting with Broony, who had come out for a smoke. She was now my coworker and thus, I guessed, my friend too, although I hadn't had time for a conversation. Or, actually, hadn't attempted one, except for a few squeaked *behind you*'s and *sorry*'s, and even those had probably been unnecessary, since Broony had been too preoccupied to respond. She was in charge of the imported espresso machine, which seemed to require a lot of tinkering and an occasional whack.

"Hey," I said, with a little wave. "Broony."

Staring at me, she dropped her cigarette to the ground and crushed it under her heel, in violation of all of Bob's rules for employee behavior on the patio. "Brunhilde," she said. "*Bitte*. If you please." She kissed Baby affectionately on both cheeks and went back inside.

Baby gave her a fluttery-finger wave. "Don't mind her," she said. "Her bark's worse than her bite." She linked her arm through mine. "The tide's out. Let's walk the jetty."

"Don't the rocks make you nervous?" To me, the jetty, beloved promenade of both townies and tourists, looked like a long, rambling opportunity to turn my ankle, fall into the water, and drown.

"I'm part goat," said Baby. "Haven't you noticed?"

"You're a randy thing," I agreed.

"You're not so bad yourself," she said and gave me a kiss on the lips, with a thrilling bit of tongue. "Come on, don't be a wuss." She began pulling me along the street, so I had no choice but to follow.

We arrived at the end of Commercial Street, a rotary with a little memorial park in the middle. Janelle and I had made a ritual of walking through it to look for the name, carved on a paving stone, of Roger's only steady boyfriend, a victim of the epidemic. Sometimes we could find it, sometimes not. I sighed, to think of Janelle and me, and Roger, and poor dead Paul Wong, whom we had never had the chance to know except in Roger's stories of their true love.

Baby, unaware of all that, kept to the sidewalk that ran alongside the Provincetown Inn, a sprawling, decrepit motel with some of the best bay views in town. I never figured out how it hadn't been taken over by a developer—it was just the sort of place that was being razed and replaced by a couple of mansions everywhere else—but until that happened its pool was a favorite Gay Family Week hangout, a parent or two sneaking a drink at the motel bar while the babies splashed around in the warm water.

An expanse of grassy wetlands, the moors, spread out before us, the palm of the Cape's hand. The jetty snaked across them to the outer dunes and Wood End lighthouse. Baby stepped onto a boulder. "Come on!" she said. "I'll hold your hand. You won't fall."

The fact that she was wearing cowboy boots with heels didn't increase my feeling of stability, but I took the hand she held out to me, and we began picking our way along the rocks and jumping over crevasses. The winter sun was low in the sky, and the clouds on the horizon glowed. A silhouetted couple paced slowly through the shallows, heads down, clamming or crabbing or some other such oceanic activity.

They looked familiar. "Oh, not again," I said. "That's Janelle and Roger."

"Are you sure?" asked Baby. "Really, it's hopeless trying to avoid anyone in this town."

"Of course I'm sure." Janelle's tufty hair haloed her head, and I would have recognized her walk anywhere.

Baby pointed to a sign at the entrance to the jetty. "Well, they're not supposed to be shell fishing here. The water's not clean." She waved her arms and called to them. "Hey! Hey!"

Janelle looked up, and Baby cupped her hands around her mouth. "Pollution!" she yelled.

Janelle and Roger turned and started walking toward us.

"I don't want them getting poisoned," Baby explained.

"Why not? Janelle would be happy if I was."

They scrambled up the rocks, pretending not to notice us. As it turned out, they weren't carrying buckets of sea creatures, just a couple of jars of murky water.

"Science project?" I asked.

Janelle glanced up. "You could call it that," she said, and I felt a brief sag of relief. The cone of silence had been breached.

"Hi," said Baby optimistically.

Janelle looked at her like she was a slimy sea creature. Me, she didn't look at, at all. After that first, automatic response to my question, she refused to acknowledge me. She and Roger continued off the jetty and onto the sidewalk.

"What's that all about, I wonder," said Baby.

"Come on," I said, tugging her hand. "It's getting too late for this walk." I hadn't wanted to do it in the first place, and encountering Janelle and Roger made the place feel toxic, and not only for shellfish. "Let's go. I told Miss Ruby I'd cook. We're having Iron Chef night— whatever's in the pantry. Tomorrow's shopping day."

"Okay, but some day you're going to walk this whole jetty with me," said Baby.

I had promised Tony I would keep watch on Miss Ruby to make sure she stuck to her resolution—or rather, Tony's—to develop better habits. Although our previous regimen had been wildly unhealthy, it had its satisfactions. It had buoyed Miss Ruby up from a depression. When I had found her—or she had found me—in the street she had been lonely and sick. Then she had begun to enjoy my company, and ordering me around, although I was sinking into a mire of confusion. Before Tony had appeared, Iron Chef night hadn't been about preparing a meal; it had been about watching a reality cooking show and eating cereal for supper. Miss Ruby favored Lucky Charms.

"What a day," I said as we approached Baby's storefront. Even though I had been going on about my evening commitment, I was kind of hoping she would invite me in. "I'm not used to getting up so early for work. And then all that walking on rocks, and running into Janelle and Roger. And Miss Ruby is cranky these days, with no cigs and real food."

But Baby didn't offer. She gave me a big hug, then *tak-tok*-ed down the walk to her door. I watched her go, and after she disappeared inside, I felt a horrible pang, as though we would be parted for months rather than hours. As though I could get myself into as much trouble by letting her go as I had by entangling myself with her.

When I Paint
My Masterpiece

And then when I got back to the cottage, Miss Ruby wasn't there. Surprised and, I realized, disappointed, since I had been feeling so virtuous about advancing our healthy lifestyle, I fed the cats and paced the kitchen, stopping every once in a while to stare into the refrigerator. I should have been figuring out my next steps in life, or at least what to fix for dinner, but my mind wasn't on either. I kept berating myself for my lack of focus and then immediately slipping off into another daydream of Baby, or speculation about Janelle and her jars of marsh water and her few words to me.

Finally there was a commotion at the door—Tony and Miss Ruby. "She made me walk all the way from the Stop & Shop," said Miss Ruby, throwing herself into her recliner. Her face was flushed and sweaty, and she was audibly wheezing, but I could see that she was pleased with herself.

"You need the exercise," said Tony.

"You just can't figure out how to fix my scooter," said Miss Ruby.

"Anyhow, it wasn't *all the way*." Tony turned to me, a concession that surprised me—her feeling the need to explain that she hadn't been torturing her friend. "She's nowhere near ready for *that*, Nella. I just kicked her out of the truck to do the last couple blocks."

"Nora," said Miss Ruby. "Jeez."

"Norma, Nella, whatever," Tony said, reverting to her usual manner. "If you want to make yourself useful for a change, the bags are out in the truck bed. Miss Ruby here has had enough for one day, I agree with her on that one." Tony gave her a little pat on the shoulder, and Miss Ruby smiled up at her. I hadn't noticed before that she had a dimple in one cheek.

Apparently, Iron Chef night, like so many of our other amusements, was now off the calendar. When I brought the bags in, Tony explained that we would go vegan for at least one day each week. "One of the kids was talking about it at meeting," she said, hacking up a turnip with a cleaver she had produced from a drawer. She had assigned me the onions. "Amazing shit. Her hair even grew in thicker." She looked over at the alopecic Miss Ruby, snoring in her chair, clearly contemplating the next steps in Miss Ruby's makeover.

When Tony had finished cooking, she shook Miss Ruby awake, which Miss Ruby didn't seem to mind at all; in fact, she seemed eager to attempt the next step in Tony's program. We sat down together to eat, plates on our laps. "All that walking works up your appetite," said Miss Ruby, nodding as though this was an effect well known to her, and popping a slice of tofu into her mouth. Her eyes widened. "What the hell, Tony?" she said. "I thought this was some kind of marshmallow."

Actually, Tony's cooking wasn't bad, if you dosed the dish with enough soy sauce and tabasco. I passed Miss Ruby the condiments. "Thanks for cooking, Tony," I said. "This tastes very healthy."

She looked pleased with the compliment and pointed her fork at me. "Well, sure, Ninny," she said. "Something healthy is always going to taste better than those boxes of chemicals you guys were addicted to."

"Bleh," said Miss Ruby, trickling tabasco onto her brown rice. "It needs sparking up."

"Your taste buds are just fried from the cigs, Rube. They'll come back eventually." Tony stood and carried her empty plate to the sink, then found her cap and squashed it onto her curls. "Sorry kiddos, but I gotta run," she said. "Enjoy."

"Meeting," explained Miss Ruby. The truck pulled away outside, and when we could no longer hear it, she hauled herself out of her chair and got a couple of beers from the refrigerator. "Low cal," she explained, before I could say anything. Settling back down and aiming the clicker at the television, she sighed. "Much better. And guess what else? I grabbed us some popsicles for dessert when Miss Drill Sergeant was busy looking at yogurt."

"Ben and Jerry's?" I asked hopefully, about our favorite brand.

"No way! Weight Watchers—I'm on a diet, girl! That Tony," said Miss Ruby. "I like to tease her, but the woman's got sense. She'll never understand, though, that you've got to sweeten things a little."

"What's your history with her, anyway?" I asked. Since her afternoon with Tony, Miss Ruby looked livelier—she even had some color in her face—and Tony herself was marginally mellower.

"You know," she said, waving her hand. "We go back. I'll tell you about it some time."

"That's what everybody in this town says. About everybody else."

"Check out the freezer," she reminded me.

And then I saw it: My next artwork. My masterpiece. And by that I wasn't thinking, necessarily, of something that would be the pinnacle of my career, but rather the transformative project. The one that would make a difference—if only to me. "Miss Ruby," I asked. "Can I paint you?"

"What? What?" said Miss Ruby, alarmed, as though I had proposed slathering her with a lead-based concoction.

"Sit for me," I said. I would start with her portrait and move on to her connections, the webs and overlapping circles of relationships. The P-town vortex as a giant mural.

"Oh, well then," said Miss Ruby. "Sure. That's something I'm good at."

Philosophy

A few days into the new year, to my utter shock, Janelle called. "Uh, hi," she said.

"You have this number!" I said.

"Research," she said. "Tracking you down was pretty simple."

"Especially since I wasn't hiding," I said, wondering where this was going. "If you remember, you threw me out on the street. With nothing. I could've, I don't know, died or something."

"Not you," said Janelle, falling silent.

Finally, annoyed, I said, "Well, bye. Thanks for getting in touch."

"No, wait," said Janelle. "This isn't easy."

"For me either!" I said. "What do you want? Why are you calling me?"

"I'm sorry I did that," she said. "Threw you out like that, without even talking about it. I'm trying to be more rational now, more philosophical."

"Philosophical," I said.

"A little," she said. "Although I don't think I can ever trust you again."

"No, of course not," I said, furious now. "I mean, how could you? After all our years together, and all I did for you, and I step out once. I mean, I feel terrible about it, okay? I'm awash in guilt, and I miss you every day. But don't tell me you never thought about it yourself. Or did it, for all I know."

She took a deep breath. "I made a resolution. I'm going to give back your sea glass. I'm sorry I took it, Nora. I know it's part of the way you were trying to support yourself. I can drop it off at the Teddy. To be honest, I don't want to come across any more stuff in the house that reminds me of you."

"Oh," I said. "Thanks. I would appreciate that." I didn't say that she could keep her old sea glass, or that I would be working on something new and bigger and more significant than craft-fair jewelry.

Janelle was still talking, her words coming quicker and louder and angrier, about her illness. Or rather, about what I had been trying to think of as her former illness, for which she had been treated and cured. "You know what? It's here too, I found out. The cancer. Do you have any idea how many women on the Cape get breast cancer?" she said, somewhat accusatorily.

"No, but—"

"I've been looking into it. There's a proven cluster. I moved here, right?—"

"We moved here," I corrected her. "Both of us."

"—and I thought I was in some pristine place. But humanity's been screwing around with the natural world, and you can't just do that and not suffer the consequences. These clusters are turning up all over the place. So Roger's going to help me. We're checking out the sea water, the aquifer."

"Aquifer?" I said.

"Fuck, Nora! Don't repeat everything I say! We're going to start a public education campaign. I've been reading up on how to do it. We'll put up posters—'Do you know what's in the water you're drinking?' Stuff like that. Then, when we've attracted some attention, we get moving. Protests. Lobbying. Start locally. Get the Stop & Shop to carry organic produce. Close down the dry cleaners."

Good for Janelle, I thought. Her plan sounded like an amazingly healthy way to channel her personal trauma into socially useful activity. But I wasn't feeling ready for rationality and health. "What dry cleaners?" I said. "Provincetown doesn't even have a functioning laundromat, which I've always wondered about, why they can't—"

"Any dry cleaners! Maybe there's one in Orleans. It doesn't matter; it's just an example. We can't let this keep happening. It's not just me."

"But it *is* you," I said. "Didn't we come here so you could rest, take care of yourself?"

"I need to do this," said Janelle. "For healing. I'm serious. I'm still so mad—well, at you, of course—"

"Of course," I said. "Why not? I just—"

"It's the whole situation." She paused and then admitted, in a low voice, "I'm afraid the anger's going to make me sick again. I need to get it out of me, get rid of it."

"But that's superstition!" I said. What, I wondered, could Janelle have been getting up to while I had been out of the house? She and I had had many conversations about the obnoxiousness of this sort of thinking. Angry men never seemed to get accused of giving themselves cancer. The repressed anger–cancer link was just a way to shut women up.

"It's how I feel, Nora. Even if it's wrong, it's deep; I can't shake it."

Public Education

Baby had never heard of a Cape Cod cancer cluster. "But that means nothing," she said, instantly convinced. "Think about it. Word gets out, and even the tourists won't drink the water. They might avoid the place altogether. And what's that, compared to somewhat fewer year-round lesbians?"

"Exactly. I've been thinking." About Janelle, and about how I had betrayed her, in her time of need. And about her research and her plans. Janelle was a geek, who had never done anything political except to watch the gay pride parade every June—because I dragged her to it, so she could cheer for me and my artist friends when we marched by. We had organized a Guerilla Girls–type collective, and we did street theater with big homemade masks, and postering and graffiti-tagging to advertise antiwar demonstrations, antiracism demonstrations—whatever was going down.

It was just unfortunate that, unlike the women I thought of as the brave revolutionaries, I was always terrified of getting caught, even with a mask on, or of offending some old lady. I had proven myself useless at passing out leaflets and engaging total strangers in rational conversation about topics we probably didn't agree about—because I didn't want them to get mad at me. Janelle's environmental campaign brought up my old worries, but at least I knew the drill.

And I owed her. Maybe, I thought, she would forgive me. "I could make some posters."

"We'll stick them up all over town!" Baby couldn't wait to get started. Her reaction wasn't quite what I had expected. I guess I had anticipated something more like polite concern. Instead, there she was, ready to throw herself into the cause. It made me feel even more caddish: women were suffering and dying up and down the Cape, and all I could think about was my ex- and current girlfriends comparing notes, whereby they would discover just how selfish and insensitive I was.

"It'll be great!" Baby continued. "Wheat paste, staple guns—just like the old days. You'll make us an inspiring image!"

"And no pink," I said. "No ribbons."

Baby held up her palm for me to slap her a high five. "The photocopying's my treat."

After that we did lots of smooching and appreciating of each other's imaginative and physical talents, and I forgot, for a while, my anxieties about Janelle, Janelle and Baby, Baby and staple guns, painting supplies and boxes, and a whole stack of other problems that often kept me up at night.

Vegan Pizza

I asked around in town, but like Baby, no one admitted to having heard anything about a Cape Cod breast-cancer cluster. I did hear a lot of stories about the mammogram machine at the hospital in Hyannis, though. "I wish they'd get a new one," Reverend Patsy confided. "I've counseled several congregation members, in terrible crisis, and then it turns out to be a false positive. Better than a false negative, I suppose." She lowered her voice. "But I think the technician is a sadist. I don't say this lightly, Nora. I can tell you from personal experience, that machine hurts more than a normal one. And then the technician claims she has to repeat the procedure because the films didn't register correctly the first time around. I've come out literally bruised."

I had run into her after my shift. The sun had broken through after a series of raw, drizzly days, and year-rounders had poured onto Commercial Street from their winter hideouts. Checking my cash register totals, Bob had been pleased. "It's Christmas come again out there," he said, rubbing his little Teddy bear between his fingers. "I don't know where they all come from." This was disingenuous: Bob had an uncanny ability to project the ebb and flow of his customers, not just from season to season but from day to day. It must have been his corporate background. Even though the Teddy was just a little coffee shop, he was getting a great return on investment.

Patsy had been sitting on the bench outside Spiritus, bundled up in a winter coat, enjoying the bright afternoon and a slice of pizza. When she saw me, she had beckoned enthusiastically and patted the space next to her. Most of my boxes were still in her office, and I had never yet made it to a Sunday service, so I felt a little guilty about sitting down

with her, but she didn't seem to have noticed my lack of faith or organization. "It's vegan," she said. "They do a mean pie with tofu mozzarella if
I call ahead. I'm sure they'd warm up a slice for you, too, if you want to
try it. It's quite good; I find I don't even miss the dairy."

"I'm sorry I haven't done anything about those boxes," I said, fending
off the vegan slice. First Tony, now Patsy. Enthusiasms blew through
Provincetown like the ever-changing cloud formations—especially during the icy fogs of winter, when the horizon line separating gray sea from
gray sky vanished, and it seemed there was nothing to focus on but self-
improvement or self-destruction. AA or the A-House bar, veganism or
Lucky Charms. "I'm not even sure what's in them. Maybe you should
just recycle them."

"Oh, for goddess's sake," she said. "I don't even notice them anymore. And I'm sure the contents are important to you in some way, or
you wouldn't have bothered packing them."

"Thanks, though," I said. She was attributing to me more self-
awareness in that chaotic moment than I deserved. "I'll get them out
of your way this week, I promise. It's time I got myself sorted out."
Reverend Patsy looked up from her pizza and nodded in agreement.

My Studio

Back at Miss Ruby's, the sound on the TV was turned down to a murmur, and in the recliner in front of it, Miss Ruby and the cats were deep into their Sunday afternoon nap—far more restorative, she believed, than their usual, weekday nap. I tiptoed past them into my room and sat down on the bed to assess my situation. The house was generally more habitable than when I had first arrived, without all the cigarette smoke and hairballs, but my room had barely enough space for a twin bed, a dresser, and a stack of boxes. The house next door, which must have been built before the invention of zoning and setbacks, was all of about five feet from Miss Ruby's cottage, blocking any possibility of light or air through my lone window.

One of my favorite paintings in the world was the one by Vincent van Gogh of his little room in Arles, with his wooden bed and red blanket, and his towel hanging on a nail next to the washstand. If I really studied it, it would start to make me dizzy. The perspective was off. One of the chairs was really big and looked like it was blocking the door. Because in fact the room wasn't a real room. It was a room in the artist's mind. Where, Van Gogh wrote to his brother, one could retreat to "rest the brain, or rather, the imagination."

It always made me want to simplify my life. But the genius Van Gogh painted outside, whereas in Provincetown it was either windy or buggy. Occasionally, it's true, you might see an artist setting up on a side street, the easel a great draw for the passing tourists. Sometimes the painting sold before it was dry. But that wasn't the way I worked.

I began sketching various rearrangements of my stuff, but transforming the space into a studio seemed hopeless. I could make jewelry sitting on my bed with a tray, if it came to that, but that was just a side-line. To create my masterpiece—and even to sketch out the posters—I needed more room.

Outside my door, I heard the thump of a bunch of cats landing on their feet. The volume on the TV went up. "Hey, Nor, you in there?" yelled Miss Ruby. "Why's the door shut?"

"I didn't want to disturb you," I said. "You looked so peaceful."

"Sunday," she agreed, with a satisfied yawn.

"I'm trying to figure out where I can paint," I said. I showed her my sketches.

"I don't see why that's such a giant problem," said Miss Ruby, handing the pages back to me. "Go out in the shed."

"What shed?" I asked.

"Jeez," said Miss Ruby. "You know, the one in back of the big yellow house."

"Jeez yourself," I said. "I can't just move into some person's shed."

"Why not?" asked Miss Ruby. "You wouldn't be the first. All these years, the summer guys are just here to party, and I don't think Joe Ruis has ever set foot in it—"

"Who?"

"—you know, the landlord."

"You have a landlord?"

"Well, yeah, Nora, did you think this dump was mine? When I buy something it won't be this old hovel. Joe owns the whole block. Probably the next one too."

"Even if he doesn't care, I wouldn't feel right. What if I get caught?"

"By who?" asked Miss Ruby, holding out her hands. I grabbed them and pulled her up from the chair. "Opportunity knocks, girl," she said, smoothing her hair and stumping off to the bathroom. "You know," she called back, "Tony might just be right about the vegan stuff. I can see in the mirror, my hair looks fluffier."

"So, beans and brown rice tonight?" I teased her. "We can mix in something green—how about brussels sprouts?"

"Not sprouts," said Miss Ruby. "The poor kitties hate the smell."

In the morning, I went to look at the shed. Despite Miss Ruby's blasé attitude toward private property, I didn't feel comfortable barging right in, so I circled the building—basically, a wooden box—and peered in the windows, which were mostly intact. I yanked on the door, half-hoping it would be locked, but it opened easily, and I found myself in a chilly, empty room with a dry sink against one wall; above it was a splintery wooden shelf scattered with shards and a few crusty pots of gray soil and dead stems. The place was dirty and probably crawling with spiders, and there was no electricity or heat or water. It wasn't Brooklyn, or even the little room in my home with Janelle, but with some scrubbing and a couple of warm sweaters, I thought I could make it work, at least in the daytime.

I spent a day carrying buckets and rags back and forth from Miss Ruby's cottage to the shed and a second day dragging over some of my boxes and arranging the contents around the room. By the end of my task, I discovered I had more drawing and painting materials than I had remembered, and in a forgotten closet in the church, Reverend Patsy found me a card table and one of those ubiquitous, white monoblock chairs.

Our poster campaign wouldn't be the first that Provincetown had seen; after Hurricane Katrina the local Buddhist nun/masseuse/restaurant hostess (for the most part, customers took her shaved head in stride) had plastered the telephone poles with "build levees not bombs" signs—but hers were modest, 3×5 requests. Baby and I were imagining something splashier. I set up my easel with a big piece of newsprint and waited for some inspiration for the posters.

It was slow, as inspiration always is. After all, I could still barely bring myself to put together the words *Janelle* and *breast cancer* in a sentence. With a piece of charcoal I sketched her in profile. Like so many women, she had never much liked her breasts: They were bigger and saggier than she thought she deserved, given how sturdy and compact the rest of her had always been. She believed their weight had stretched down her aureoles until they were shaped like teardrops—an exaggeration. But who sees herself as she truly is? Not even Janelle. I drew other profiles: mine, Baby's, Miss Ruby's, imaginary women with all sizes and shapes of breasts. "Most women who get breast cancer have no risk factors," I scrawled over the drawings. "Except living on this earth. Clean water now!"

"Our first installment!" said Baby when I unrolled it to show her. "It's beautiful!" She planted a big purpley-red kiss on my check and re-rolled the poster. "I'll bring it over to Dorothy and get her to print us up a bunch." Dorothy owned a T-shirt shop. "This is good timing— slow season, she'll be bored. After New Year's she starts getting ready for summer, her studio turns into a twenty-four-hour baby-dyke sweatshop, and she wouldn't stop silk-screening to run over her own grandmother."

Wheat Paste

I started assembling the materials for a night of illicit postering. I put up a big pot of wheat paste to simmer on the stove while Miss Ruby and Tony were absorbed in a junior high school field-hockey tournament on local cable, so I didn't think they would pay much attention to anything I was doing. "Sticks! Sticks!" Tony was shouting. "The Nauset girls are clobbering Danny Pereira! That ref ought to be fired! He shouldn't be allowed around kids!"

"We're creaming them anyway," said Miss Ruby. "Come look, Nora!" she called. "What are you so busy with in there? Another new diet?"

"Not exactly," I said.

"Flour and water?" said Tony. "That's no diet. You'd be as scurvied up as the Franklin expedition inside a week."

"So what is it, Nora?" persisted Miss Ruby.

"Ninny's secret recipe," said Tony.

"Nora," Miss Ruby corrected.

"Actually, it *is* kind of a secret," I said.

"But not from us, right?" said Miss Ruby.

Cheering erupted on the TV, and Tony leaped up and pumped both fists in the air. "Goal! Pereira scores again! Ha! Ha! This is what that ref doesn't get. And those Nauset players. All the kids have to wear the same uniform, and if it's a skirt, it's a skirt. Otherwise, where's your team cohesion?"

"It's to put up posters," I explained. "About breast cancer."

"Breast cancer," said Tony.

"Because of the cluster, you mean?" said Miss Ruby.

"Wait a minute; you said you didn't know about any cluster."

"I don't like to think about that stuff," said Miss Ruby. "We've got to live here, so what can you do?"

Tony gave her friend a withering stare. Then she turned to me. "Nora," she said. "Tell us more."

"It's not that big a deal," I said. I could just see it: first Tony and Miss Ruby, and next thing I knew, the Town Crier guy who ran around all summer in a sweaty Pilgrim outfit having his picture taken with tourists in front of Town Hall would be ringing his bell and announcing who was behind the posters, and the police would be knocking on my door in the middle of the night. "There's not that much to it."

Slowly, Tony untucked her T-shirt and pulled it up to her neck, revealing a bony, scarified chest. "Put me out of commission for a while," she said. "A couple years, actually. And your friends—some come through. Some don't." She jerked her head toward Miss Ruby.

"Don't I know it," I said. She had caught me.

Miss Ruby looked away, her cheeks slowly turning a remarkably lurid red.

"Yeah, that's how she got her name," said Tony. "Blushing for her sins."

"Didn't I say I was sorry?" Miss Ruby muttered. A Siamese jumped up on her lap and began howling as Miss Ruby stroked her. "Yes, you like that, don't you?" she purred at the cat. She looked at me. Sighed. "Nora, my dear, I want you to know, it was hella complicated. Tony's in twelve step for a reason."

Tony glared at her. "The program's anonymous, remember? That's hitting below the belt, Rube."

"Just don't wreck my cooking pot with your paste stuff," Miss Ruby told me.

Tagging

The wheat paste was in the refrigerator, the posters printed, and the night moonless, with a high wind rattling the trees and rolling garbage cans and anything else that was not tied down along the street. Perfect weather. No one would bother to investigate a little extra racket outside. The plan was for Miss Ruby to transport our supplies on her scooter while Tony, riding pillion, kept a lookout. Baby and I would do the actual postering.

Baby and I had finished stowing the paste, brushes, and staple gun on the scooter in Miss Ruby's driveway when Baby felt around in her coat pocket and, opening her fist, revealed a squashed joint and a book of matches. "Have a hit?" she asked.

"I don't think so. It makes me paranoid," I said. "I'm anxious enough already."

"This stuff's different," said Baby, lighting the joint and taking a deep drag. She cupped her hand under my chin and tilted my face up to hers—as Janelle had once done, in quite different circumstances. Baby's lips on mine, she opened my mouth with her tongue and exhaled into my lungs. Pulling away, she took another hit and handed the joint to me. Figuring I had nothing left to lose, I puffed on it, and we shared it back and forth a few more times, until finally she dropped the spent reefer and ground it out under a new white sneaker. Even she had had to admit that the *tak-tok* of her boots was just too distinctive. "Now," she said, "we're ready to go."

"Ready," I said giddily.

Baby looked at me with a slow smile. "Feeling more relaxed, sweetness?" she asked.

I nodded.

"What did I tell you? Look at those stars," she said. "They're as big as Christmas balls."

Baby took my hand and led me down the street, and Miss Ruby and Tony passed us on the scooter, honking and waving. In that buoyant moment, I believed that the cluster didn't exist, that no one would notice our posters on their property, that the Cape aquifer was pure and clean, and that Baby and I would go back to her place after our escapade and have great sex to the crashing of waves and the hooting of foghorns. And at least some things turn out the way you imagine.

We quickly developed a routine. Miss Ruby would pull up to a light pole, trash can, or other promising object, and I would unroll a poster and hold it in place while Baby slapped on the wheat paste, which she mostly managed to do without dripping it all over our jackets and shoes, or gunned it with the stapler. We started in the East End, sticking up a poster every block or two, and it was late and cold enough so that we didn't encounter anyone except an incurious cigarette smoker/dog-walker and a woman with several wooly scarves wrapped around her head, who was completely absorbed in cursing out her invisible companion.

When we reached the middle of town, though, someone turned a corner in front of Baby and me, bright blonde pigtails glowing. "Broony!" whispered Baby. "Let's say hi."

"Are you kidding? After we've gotten this far with no one seeing?" I grabbed Baby's arm. "Let her keep going and maybe she won't notice us." And in fact, as we ambled behind her, she turned the next corner off Commercial Street. "Phew," I said.

Baby said nothing.

After we put up the last poster, on a light pole across from the post office, Miss Ruby putted off to take Tony home. Baby reached into her pocket again. "I brought us a surprise, for a grand finale!" she said. "Check this out." She pulled out a can of purple spray paint and rattled it at me.

"Brilliant!" I said. I admit my judgment was not what it should have been. Postering signposts and light poles: okay. Tagging the Green Teddy patio: not okay.

We took turns writing our message, passing the spray can back and forth and giggling: "F-U-C-K C-A-N-C-E-R!" Then we stepped back to admire our work. "Janelle is going to be amazed when she sees all this!" I said.

"You didn't tell her about the posters?" asked Baby.

"Nope—I wanted it to be a surprise. It's been so hard to figure out how to help her—but she was really into the idea of an environmental campaign. She'll love this."

Baby answered me with a kiss. "You're a good person," she said. "Don't let anyone tell you different."

The next morning, Baby said, "I can't wait to see Bob's reaction."

My head was still fuzzy. Baby and I had fallen into bed feeling so pleased with ourselves, and then with each other, that it hadn't dawned on us that the rest of the world might not share our insouciance. We had persuaded ourselves that the patio looked fantastic, better than ever. "Come with me to the Teddy," I offered. "I'm on first thing."

Broony wasn't scheduled to work but she popped up exactly in time for my shift—for the sole purpose, I'm sure, of ratting me out. "It was the new girl," she announced as she and Baby and I converged on Bob, who was standing in the street and staring at his patio, frantically stroking GT. "I saw on my way home from the gym."

This seemed suspicious. Confronted, I said, "The gym? In the middle of the night? Brunhilde, were you spying on us?"

"You think Germans are spies? You are an American bigot!" Broony pointed at me triumphantly. "'The middle of the night.' You betray yourself! Off to jail! Baby will miss you, for sure. Or perhaps she will not! Perhaps she will have other preoccupations."

"Broony, really!" said Baby.

"Nobody goes to jail for defacing a patio," I said. "In this country they fine you for that, if anything."

Bob put Green Teddy back in his vest pocket. "Sorry to break up this lovely gathering," he said. "In this country they *fire* you for that."

"Oh, come on, Babs. I'll clean it up," I offered, although I should have known better than to use his drag name at that moment. "I got carried away. But I'll fix it."

"*Bob*," he corrected me, adopting his most corporate manner. "To you, *Mr. Robert Johnson*. I don't think you're taking this seriously, Nora. But if I find you near my patio again I *will* have you picked up, for trespassing and property damage. And I'm hiring a pro. This mess is going to be totally erased." It wasn't that Bob didn't endorse our cause, of preventing breast cancer and environmental destruction. He was a person with women friends and a conscience. And like all Provincetown businesspeople, he was also, rather confusingly, wary both of any issue that had the potential to drive away his customers and of the crowding and overdevelopment he profited from. "The Teddy can't get involved in these slogans and things. I hate to let you go," he said, relenting a little, "but what were you thinking?"

"It was for Janelle," I tried to explain. "And then me and Baby—"

Baby interrupted me. "She wasn't thinking anything, Bob! The spray paint was my idea!"

"Not true; Nora is the one!" Broony yelled. "I saw!"

"Ladies, ladies," said Bob. "Peace." He pointed at Broony. "You. Calm down." Then he pointed at Baby. "You. Don't try to cover up for her." He pointed at me. "And you. You can pay for the cleanup."

"I guess it was kind of my fault," I admitted. "It was stupid. I'm really sorry, Mr. Robert—"

"No, no, no!" Baby said. "This is wrong!"

"Not wrong," muttered Broony.

"I thought it would be fun," said Baby. "I'll pay."

"But I got into it as much as you," I told her. I didn't want her paying. Letting my girlfriend get mixed up in my finances, I had learned, just led to problems. I didn't have the cash to compensate Bob all at once, but we set up a plan for me to pay him in weekly installments until Memorial Day. My brief barista days were over.

Stop & Shop

So that's how I ended up working behind the deli counter at the Stop & Shop.

In fact, it was a far more practical job than the one I had had at the Teddy—more hours, better pay, more predictable coworkers. I had anticipated a less interesting atmosphere, but that was before I understood that hardly anyone came through Provincetown without making at least one trip to the grocery store. In the summer, the undisciplined children of straight couples scampered down the aisles pushing shopping carts. They caromed off Margot, buying Wheaties for her grandkids; off arthritic fishermen buying shrimp rings; off bikinied lesbians buying maraschino cherries for Manhattans on the roof deck; off freshly showered, sweet-smelling gay men buying pork tenderloins for the grill; off the day manager, looming large in her purple apron, who stopped them in their tracks: "Quit it, ya brats!" In the winter, for locals, the store was a major social hub.

Sometimes, as I handed over Janelle's order of feta cheese or potato salad, I got the feeling that she pitied me for having slid down so many rungs on the social ladder, but I reminded myself that the vocation of the artist is quite different from that of the tech whiz, and that I was fortunate, in Provincetown's resort economy, to have a steady day job that didn't involve cleaning hotel toilets. She didn't see herself as at all implicated in my situation. "I guess you meant well, but defacing every surface in town wasn't a great way to get people to trust us. And taking that sort of risk just isn't like you. Did whatsis talk you into it?"

I ignored her implication that I was hopelessly timid and easily pressured. "I was moving out of my comfort zone," I explained, trying out a phrase I had heard from Tony. "Anyway, the Teddy patio is hardly every surface in town. And Bob's forgiven me. We have an arrangement, and I go over there for a latte every week. He even asked if I had an extra poster he could hang up in the shop. He thinks it'll be a collectors' item."

"So now you're the next Keith Haring?"

"Maybe." I doubted it, though. My new job, combined with my exchange with Miss Ruby of services and a token payment for room and board, and my studio squat, enabled me to support myself—which was, after all, what I had wanted in the first place, and what had led to my meeting Baby, the crisis with Janelle, and everything that had followed. The income made my life more predictable, and it kept me in art supplies.

But it curtailed the time I had for the actual art. Standing on my feet for an entire shift was exhausting, and it was too dark and cold to work in the shed in the evenings when I got home. I often ended up spending my days off cleaning and running errands for Miss Ruby, and when my chores were done, I couldn't resist playing around with Baby. We spent sweet afternoons having sex and napping and cooking dinners for two. She led me over the trails that wound through the dunes and out to the bay. We watched seals haul out to sun themselves on the sand and were harassed by gulls. One morning I even let her lead me all the way across the jetty, after she agreed to wear her wheat-pasting sneakers rather than her cowboy boots.

She asked from time to time when I would design another poster, but since Janelle had shown so little enthusiasm for the attempt Baby and I had made to start her awareness and action campaign, and the outcome for me had been so completely disastrous, I decided to postpone that. Having made such a fuss about needing a studio—if only to myself—I was embarrassed to have used it so rarely. My next day off would be spent there, I announced to Baby, no matter how tempting her affections or how lovely the weather. I had to get started on my mural. "That's right, sweetheart, you do your thing," said Baby.

"I mean, I do want to see you," I backtracked. I didn't like her agreeing so easily not to see me.

"Go to your shed," she said. "I know you artistic types. If you're not doing your work, you get all anxious and guilty and become a general drag to be around."

"Oh no, not that!" I said, trying to make light of her comment—but the last thing I wanted was for Baby to decide I was a drag, so I was stuck with my resolution.

The Mural

January in New England is mostly cold and dreary, but every once in a while there's a freakish day that reminds you that in some parts of the world, it's spring. I pulled on an extra sweater and propped open the door of the shed with a moribund potted plant, to let in the fresh breeze. The day was almost cloudless, except for a few wisps of cirrus near the horizon, ornaments that made the blue around them seem bluer, and you could actually feel rays of the sun warming your face or your back.

I had bought a tall roll of newsprint, and I measured long sheets and pinned them up around all four walls. Then I sat in the doorway in my wobbly plastic chair and stared at the paper and thought about the landscape and the seascape, how the birds see them and how to represent them. Sea grass, beach roses, poison ivy, and cranberries. Birches and gnarled, wind-stunted pines. Skunks, raccoons, coyotes, foxes, and deer. One year, a bear—he swam the canal and ambled up to Provincetown, snatching food from people's garbage cans all the way. A crosshatch of streets, the slash of Route 6, dashes of color—cars, gardens, houses. Foam-capped waves, seals, diving ducks and skimming ducks, whales and dolphins. Ferries, scallopers, pleasure boats, and kayaks. Fishes, pebbles, lobsters, clams, and kelp.

Extending over it all is the net of human relationships. I'm no naturalist, no Henry David Thoreau tramping the length of the Cape. I'm from the city, and I'm interested in the people, and how the hand of the Cape gathers everyone and everything together in its palm.

At New York gay pride marches, I had heard the chant of the P-town contingent: "0-2-657 / Provincetown is just like heaven." Medieval painters used gold leaf to represent heaven, so I started by dabbing flecks and stipples all over my paper, before I even laid down the boundaries of land and sea. The geography would be a wash of color over it: blue for the sea; green for the land, a topographical map. My portraits of people and animals would nestle among the textures.

I was pleased with my day's work, even though I didn't have a lot to show for it that would mean much to anyone else. But my vision was clearing; I was getting a sense of a way forward, the rhythm and the shape of the piece. I called Baby to tell her about my productive afternoon, but she didn't answer, so I left a voice mail. I assumed that, as often, she was in her shop.

But she was not in her shop. She was swimming.

When she called back, she was full of admiration for my efforts. "You're so diligent!" she said. "It always amazes me, how you people get things done. I'd never have the discipline—some new possibility would come up, and I'd go for that instead."

She was right about herself. Baby wasn't an artist; she was an appreciator: A sunset, the clear cold sea, a ripe mango on sale at the Stop & Shop. The pleasant click of her boot heels on the sidewalk. The view from her window. Me, in her bed.

Thus, her afternoon: taking advantage of the clear sky and the warm sun, she had driven out to Herring Cove. I could just see her, in her wet suit and red cowboy boots, with her pink towel and her yellow-daisy bathing cap. On such a nice day, she hadn't been the only one on the beach, and as she ambled down to the water, Broony had appeared beside her. "Race you to the lifeguard stand," Broony offered.

"I'm not into competition, Broony; you know that."

"You are strong, Baby; you might beat me," Broony tempted her. She dove, and Baby dove after her, stroking wildly. She lost, of course, since she had no interest in winning. But it was fun, and when they had had enough of racing, they hauled themselves out onto the sand, like the seals, panting and dripping. Broony congratulated herself by raising both arms in a V for Victory sign and turning around slowly for the admiration of all. Baby spread out her pink towel.

"You like to swim?" Broony asked her.

"Sure," said Baby.

And Broony said, "Train with me. I want to swim at the beginning of the summer, in the Swim for Life. I want to win it!"

Baby laughed. "But Broony, the Swim for Life isn't a race!"

It's a fund-raiser, for AIDS care. The swimmers collect donations from their friends, and then they swim the mile or so from Long Point to the Boatslip beach. Lesbians in kayaks and rowboats accompany them and keep them on course, and drag queens dressed as cheerleaders and waving pompoms welcome them at the finish line. Since it takes place on the weekend before Memorial Day, it's a time for the town to take a last look around, collect itself, and get ready for the long hours and frantic pace of the summer.

"For me it is," said Broony. "Everything is so. They announce who is first to the finish, do they not? That person will be me." She flexed a bicep, and accommodatingly, Baby gave it a squeeze. "Not just for the girls. For all the racers."

"Swimmers," Baby corrected her. "Tell you what: I'll train with you, but just for the hell of it. I'll swim the Swim; you can race it if you want."

"Deal!" said Broony. "We will make a good pair."

As Baby described her delightful, energizing swim with Broony and their training regimen, I became more and more appalled. "Baby, how could you do this to me? Broony is my *enemy*! She got me fired! And I thought the winter swimming was a special thing between us. Not something you'd do with anyone who just happens to show up."

"You own the ocean?" said Baby, annoyed.

Suddenly, awfully, I found myself in the middle of our first fight. Baby not only didn't have a jealous bone in her body; she didn't seem to understand the concept. And she abhorred conflict. "This is silly," she said. "Let's talk tomorrow, when we've both forgotten all about this. I had a nice day, and I want to sit in my living room with a glass of wine and watch the tide go out."

Sit in her living room with a glass of wine and watch the tide go out— so she could fill the vista before her with fantasies of Broony and her biceps! "Oh, Baby!" I cried, collapsing into my plastic chair. It turned over sideways and dumped me onto the cold, dirt floor. A cloud blew in and blocked the sun. "I won't be able to forget about it!"

"Tomorrow, sweetness," she said and hung up the phone.

I looked up at the painting I had done that day. What a mess.

Miss Ruby Sits

I decided to concentrate on the portraits. On an afternoon when Tony had taken Miss Ruby on a walk to the center of town and back that had left Miss Ruby too exhausted even to turn on the TV, I invited her to come up to the studio.

"More walking?" she said.

"Oh, come on, Miss Ruby," I said. "It's just across the yard. And once we get there, you can rest. I have a chair."

Grumpily, she picked up a cat in one arm and put the other arm around my shoulders, and with her leaning on me the way she had when we first met, we stumbled up to the studio. I pulled out the chair for her. "It's tippy," she complained, trying to settle the squirming cat on her lap. She had grabbed the wrong animal, though—it wasn't one of the huggy ones—and finally it gave a yowl, dug its claws into her thigh, and leaped off. It tried to slink out the door, a jerry-rigged thing made of two French windows that didn't quite meet in the middle, but finding it couldn't fit through, the cat curled up in front of the door in a sullen heap. "Ow," said Miss Ruby, rubbing her leg. "Goddamn thing."

"Just try to relax," I said, pulling out my drawing pad and pencils.

"Now what?" said Miss Ruby.

"Now I'm going to draw you," I coaxed her. "You promised you'd sit for me."

"I thought you brought me here just for a look around," Miss Ruby wheezed. "Use your imagination, can't you?"

"Don't be such a crank; it's not the same."

80

She pulled an inhaler out of her pocket and sucked on it a few times. "Guess not," she agreed. "I swear, that Tony's going to be the death of me. I was breathing better when I was on the cigs."

"Oh, no, you don't," I said. "After all your effort, you don't want to start that up again."

She sighed. "They were a comfort, you know. Like little friends."

"Well, now you have me and Tony."

Miss Ruby rolled her eyes.

"Don't you think it's kind of insulting to compare us to Marlboros?"

"Little friends," she repeated.

There's an interesting thing that happens between artist and sitter, at least in my experience. While the artist concentrates on the drawing or painting, not saying much, the sitter loses awareness of the purpose of the encounter. Her mind wanders, and she begins to talk freely. "So, Miss Ruby," I prompted her, to distract her from her cigarette jones, "what brought you to Provincetown?"

"What brought me? Nothing *brought* me, unless you mean my mother, carrying me for nine months! Girl, I'm Provincetown born and bred."

"You're kidding," I said, looking at her through a squint, to get another perspective. "I didn't know that."

"Well, not many can say that, these days. We were what you might call traditional, my dad either out fishing or out carousing, my mom keeping house, cooking—*she* was the real support of the family. Nobody could make the *caldo verde* like her—for a while, she made a business of it, fixing giant pots of the stuff every weekend and delivering it to restaurants. My dad and me, we never got tired of it."

"What did you call it?"

"Kale soup!" said Miss Ruby. "You've lived here all these months and haven't had it yet?"

"You're Portuguese?"

"Well, sure," said Miss Ruby. "Ruby Cabral. What else would I be?"

"But aren't you, you know . . ." I stopped, realizing that I had assumed all this time that she was a lesbian, although one who was old and had had enough of the scene. But we had never actually had a conversation about it.

"Gay?" said Miss Ruby. "I would have thought that was obvious too."

"Well, yeah," I said. "I thought—"

"Nora," said Miss Ruby. "I thought you were smarter than this. Is there some kind of law that says you can't be both? My mom took in guests every summer—artists, gays, straights, whoever could pay the rent. Several years in a row, I remember, we had this couple, older ladies, as I thought then, although they were probably about the age I am now.

"They came every summer to paint, for a couple of weeks. I imagine they didn't get but that much time off from their jobs. They'd be out there every day with their easels, around town or down by the pier. Then at night I'd hear them partying together.

"Partying, in that old house," she mused. "The walls were like paper. *You* might think the little cottages around here are so pretty," Miss Ruby said accusingly.

"But they are, aren't they?" I said, wanting to defend myself, although I wasn't sure from what.

"Sure, with their weathered shingles and flowers in the front yard— my mother would put me to work as soon as we had a thaw, weeding, watering. But they were drafty and cold in the winter, and up some rickety stairway that was more like a ladder, those stuffy bedrooms! It's no wonder I've got the asthma now. Everybody on top of each other— parents, kids, borders. Some don't like all the tearing down and putting up and gutting and rehabbing that goes on around here, but I'll tell you something, I say, *Go to it!*

"The beds my mother put in for the guests, they were really more like cots. Thinking back, Nora, I truly don't know how those old girls managed it. They were quite a substantial pair, you know?

"A real inspiration," Miss Ruby concluded. "I think of them often now that I'm a little older and substantial myself." She patted her belly proudly with both hands, and I made a fast sketch in a corner of the paper, to capture the gesture. "There were a lot of years when I had a helluva grand time."

She stood and gathered the hissing cat into her arms. "And that's enough for now, okay? I was hoping to get a nap in before supper."

"How about kale soup?"

"It would be nice, wouldn't it? I even have the secret family recipe. But not tonight, unless there's such a thing as veggie linguica sausage. Which I doubt."

"Tony's coming?"

"Yeah. For vegan night."

Dyke Drama

Sylvie at the post office handed my mail across the counter, grasped my hand, and asked, "How's your friend? Ms. Janelle Elizabeth Burnside, Box 1057, I think it is? All those express packages from New York—she's got one waiting for her right now. I bet she telecommutes; so many of them do now—"

"Good, I guess," I said. "I haven't really seen her—"

"Oh, my, I know what that's like," said Sylvie. "I see it all the time. People move here together and then a few months later—"

"She's fine, Sylvie," I interrupted. I knew Sylvie's name only because it was embroidered on her uniform shirt, so I couldn't figure out why we were having this conversation. "Nice weather we're having."

"You like these gray days? Well, she must miss you," said Sylvie. "That's probably it—some people get morbid. She was all on about the cancer. Cancer, cancer, cancer—she came in here asking about it and writing everything down. If anyone had heard of a cluster and who's had it and what type. She said she was taking a survey. The other customers were a little disconcerted, to be honest. Some don't like to talk about it, outside the family. I sure don't. My mother, you know—"

"I'd like a book of stamps," I said. "I'm sorry to hear about your mother."

"Thank you, dear, it was a long time ago. But you know, you never get over a thing like that. I don't go a day without thinking of her, not one. Maybe not even an hour." She rummaged around in her drawer. "I have some of those pink ribbon stamps in here someplace. I hear your girlfriend was stage four by the time they caught it."

"That's nonsense, Sylvie," I said, gathering up my junk mail and the packet of stamps. "Please don't keep repeating this stuff. Janelle is a very private person."

"Not my impression," called Sylvie as I stalked off.

Maybe Sylvie was right, and Janelle wasn't private at all. Maybe she had changed. Maybe I was the only person in town who didn't know every detail of her existence. Later that week, during my next shift, she appeared at the deli counter and asked for a half pound of olive loaf, sliced thin. "Roger's here again?" I asked.

"I told him it's full of carcinogens, but he wants what he wants. And does everyone in this town have to know every little thing? What do you care about who's staying at my house?" said Janelle.

"He's my friend," I pointed out.

"*My* friend, you mean. Like that awful woman in the post office, trying to weasel out why we'd moved here, and why I was so interested in cancer. I told her I have six months to live." Then she added quickly, "Roger's taking a semester's leave from teaching and coming up here to help me with the environmental campaign—like a real friend. Unlike some people, who walked out on me."

"Wait—what? I walked out on you?" I probably should have ignored her rewrite of our history, but I couldn't let this go. "You physically pushed me out of the house and into the street!"

"Yes—because you cheated! You were getting it on—"

I tried to interrupt her. "Maybe, but—"

"You can't deny that, Nora! And in our home!"

"I'm not denying it! I'm not denying anything! I fucked up bad, okay? But I never meant to hurt you."

"Who cares what you meant!"

"I thought it would just be a momentary—I didn't think you'd notice," I admitted.

"You didn't think I'd *notice*? So you were planning to lie, on top of cheating? Listen, I kicked you out, you walked out. Whatever. Whatever! It's insignificant. You're gone."

"I'll come—" I started, although I had no idea what I was about to offer to do.

"No, Nora! Fuck you! And your fat blonde friend!"

I stared at her in shock. A few people had lined up behind her while we were talking, but they had started to look uncomfortable and drift off. I guess it's more satisfying to hear the dish on the latest dyke drama at the Stop & Shop secondhand than to get caught up in it when you're just trying to get your errands done. Wrapping the olive loaf in white paper, I held it out to Janelle with, I thought, admirable professional courtesy. I used to take such comfort in her cheerful calmness and rationality. The walk she took every morning to sort things out in her head before she started her day. Her interest in and encouragement of everyone she met.

She snatched the package out of my hand. "Great. Thanks. Let Roger get cancer too!"

Jellyfish

A squib in the *Provincetown Banner* announced that because of the recent increase in outbreaks of scary mosquito-borne diseases like Eastern Equine Encephalitis and West Nile virus, the state Department of Public Health was recommending that southeastern Massachusetts and Cape Cod towns begin regular insecticide spraying as soon as the weather warmed up. Actually, I hadn't noticed the announcement, but Broony had pointed it out to Baby during their weekly swim. Broony, that idiot, had been pleased about the spraying, because she didn't want her training program interrupted by illness.

"I hope she gets stung by a jellyfish," I told Baby as she touched up her lipstick. We were in my shed. Since my session with Miss Ruby had gone so well, I had thought I would try Baby, too. Always game, she had agreed, although not without hesitation, to pose as a swimmer. "You could have picked a more attractive outfit," she said. "More dignified. But follow your vision, my dear." I had seated her in the plastic chair in her wet suit and red boots, pink towel across her shoulders, yellow-daisy bathing cap at the ready in her hand. She was able to sit quite still, yet naturally. Baby's pink, red, and yellow, I decided, would appear nowhere else in the work.

"Oh, you," said Baby. "The jellyfish here aren't the poison kind. We just get the little white ones, and not until August."

"The spraying is just the sort of thing Janelle was warning about. There has to be a better way to prevent horrible diseases than by drenching everything with carcinogens, where they leach into the water and cause yet other horrible diseases."

"Absolutely!" said Baby, enthusiastically, without breaking her pose. "Posters, phase two! I'm up for it. We'll stick to mailboxes and telephone poles this time."

Federal and corporate property, I thought. "No, I'm thinking we start a petition," I said. "To get it on the town meeting agenda."

Baby sighed. And she wasn't a big sigher.

I wondered if it had indeed been a mistake to put her in her swimming outfit. Perhaps it was reminding her at that very moment of her swimming companion, Broony. "What?" I asked.

"Petition, meeting—it sounds boring."

"It won't be boring, Baby!" I insisted. "We'll hang out on Commercial Street with clipboards and talk to everybody. Community organizing—we bring it to a vote. The spraying stops, once and for all. Eventually, the water clears up, and we can all stop paying for Poland Spring."

"And what will your employer think of that?" teased Baby.

"Screw Stop & Shop," I said carelessly. "They have a monopoly on *food*. What do they have to worry about?"

"Screw you too," she said, standing and stretching and knocking the plastic chair onto its side. "Get over here."

I ended up feeling glad I had found a nice throw rug, which padded the floor.

Dreams R2B Realized

The thing is, my relationship with Janelle had not ended because I didn't love her anymore, and her renewed rejection caused a terrible stab of pain. I had thought that maybe, if I produced a really great result for her environmental protest, she would be at least slightly grateful—slightly in my debt. The balance would shift.

I looked into the town bylaws and discovered that we needed only one hundred signatures to get an item on the agenda for a special town meeting, which sounded manageable. I bought clipboards and pens at the hardware store and decided to spend a few hours in front of Town Hall on my next afternoon off. Baby was working in her shop, Miss Ruby was feeling wheezy, and Tony was driving one of her sponsees to the dentist, so I was on my own. I figured that if I got a good start, it would encourage the others when it was their turn.

Margot was performing in front of Town Hall with a new sign: "Dreams R2B Realized!" Not wanting to compete, I waited for a break. Margot shook my hand and signed with a flourish, so I had an outstanding first signature. I felt encouraged: if Margot understood the issues, others would too; the petition drive would be successful, and Janelle would stop being so angry—at the world, and at me in particular. Of course it would also be a step toward cleaning up the Cape environment—but I'm not sure the political-ecological impact was uppermost in my mind. Following their troubadour's example, a couple of people in Margot's audience signed too—although it later turned out that they were tourists and not eligible to vote.

Then I saw Patsy. "Hey, Rev!" I called. She was sure to be good for a signature. Maybe even a sermon. According to the sign board outside the church, the previous week had been blessing of the animals/vegan Sunday. She might want some related topics. "Sign my petition?"

She crossed the street eagerly. "Good for you," she said. "Where do I sign? What's it for? The Human Rights Campaign?"

"No, it's not anything gay," I said, although my feeling was that only a straight person would consider the Human Rights Campaign gay. The group had a storefront in town that sold anything that could be emblazoned with its equal-sign logo, from oven mitts to truck flaps. Some anarchistic person had printed up a lot of stickers with an alternative, greater-than sign, but those never caught on, because who can remember from algebra class which way the little dagger points for "greater-than" and which way for "less-than" (besides Janelle, that is) — so some people displayed the stickers backward, and then others thought they were antigay and ripped them down. Reverend Patsy looked disappointed, and I explained: mosquito-borne diseases, pesticide spraying, water pollution, cancer. Her face slowly turned pink, as if her collar was suddenly too tight.

"This petition presents an ethical dilemma," she said.

"What?" I said. "It's just to start a discussion."

"But what's there to discuss? How can we deprive people of protection?" she asked. "We know for sure that the mosquitoes cause disease, and the threat is imminent. The cancer connection is much less certain."

"It is not, Patsy! I bet you have women with it in your congregation!"

"I do, yes," she said. "But what makes you think it's because of this?"

"When was the last time you drank P-town water?" I asked.

"Oh, that," said Patsy. "That's a rumor. People just don't like the taste. The testing shows the water's safe."

"And you believe that," I said.

"And the spraying, too. It's for the greater good," said Reverend Patsy. "I always sign petitions, Nora, but I can't in good conscience join you on this one."

"All right, I can respect that," I said. But Patsy wouldn't go away. A few people stopped to see what was going on, and she shooed them off.

"Don't you have something to do over at your church?" I prodded her. She seemed to spend more time wandering Commercial Street than she did in her office.

"Wait here a minute," she said. "Don't go away." A couple of dish-washers from a nearby restaurant, Moldovan college students who had outstayed their summer visas, had come outside for a break, and she approached them, shaking her head and pointing at their cigarettes. "Very bad," she enunciated. "Bad. Get sick."

The students laughed. "Whatever, bitch," said one. The other pulled at the neck of his T-shirt, clearly fascinated by Patsy's clerical collar.

"We have a quit-smoking group at the church," she pushed on, real-izing their English was more fluent than she had assumed. "You are welcome to join us."

"Church! No way, bitch," said the student, who apparently thought this was the correct American form of address for an older woman. "Church don't like the gays. Don't like the boys like us."

"No, this is a different type of church!" Patsy tried to explain, but they turned their backs on her. Finishing their cigarettes and dropping them on the sidewalk, they went back inside. Patsy pushed the butts to-gether with the side of her sneaker and, taking a tissue from her pocket, gathered them up and put them in the trash. She rummaged in her backpack until she found a small bottle of hand sanitizer and squirted a blob into her palm.

"Be prepared!" she said, rubbing her hands together with effortful cheeriness. "It's so bad for them, especially at their age." I felt a sudden respect for her well-meant interventions, but then she turned her atten-tion back to me. "Don't you believe in climate change?"

This was infuriating. Janelle had convinced me that her cancer was a result of man's environmental depredations, and now Reverend Patsy was looking at me as though I were some sort of Neanderthal Republican. "Of course I do! That's the whole point!"

"I don't see it. Suddenly there are all these new diseases. We have to respond somehow, don't we? Maybe spraying isn't the best way, I admit that." Tears sprung to her eyes. "But if it saves even one life I'm for it!"

"But what about women with cancer? What about Janelle?"

"What about our vulnerable children and elders?" she cried. "I'm sorry to say this, but Janelle was ill before you got here. Now, she's getting better."

"I know that! But I'm talking about our environment, here, on Cape Cod. And the women of the future! What about their environment? Their lives?" I tried crossing the street but she followed, and being trailed by a minister turning people away was doing nothing for my petition.

She looked at me sorrowfully. "You're a friend, Nora," she said. "But your action is just terribly wrongheaded."

"Right," I said. "I would have thought you'd be in favor of democratic debate."

"Democracy is a value. But so is the interconnected web of all existence of which we are a part," she recited.

Margot started singing again—you would have thought that at least one drag queen, if that's what Margot was, could come up with something more original for an encore than "My Way," although I guessed the alternative was "I Will Survive," which is equally annoying. Discouraged by the challenge of competing with both Margot and Reverend Patsy, I put my pens in my shirt pocket and tucked the clipboard under my arm. "Okay, I give up," I told Reverend Patsy. No way was I going to rush to get my boxes out of her study, I decided, and I wasn't attending her church service, either.

The Shopping Cart Protest

"You must've got off on the wrong foot," said Miss Ruby.

"You try it, then," I said.

"Okay," she said. Tony's walking and nutrition program had started to take effect. Miss Ruby was getting out more, and she had recently abandoned her gray sweats for a new uniform of denim overalls and red T-shirts. She had had Dorothy at the T-shirt shop make several with her name spelled out on the back in rhinestones: MISS RUBY. "Town Hall was the wrong place to try to get signatures," she said. "It's all day-trippers. You need to go where the townies are."

When it was time for my next shift, she gave me a ride on the back of her scooter, and while I went into the store, she hung around in the parking lot with her clipboard. Maybe she was right about Town Hall, because she collected fifteen signatures in front of the Stop & Shop before she got bored and left.

She was very pleased with herself when I got home. "Now you've got something to work with," she said, having become an expert. "The first ones are the hardest; nobody wants to stick their neck out."

"Great, only eighty-four more to go," I said, "counting the one I got from Margot." Calling the meeting was going to be more difficult than I had thought.

"And listen to this—I got a ton of compliments on my shirt; I bet I could get more customers for Dorothy without half-trying."

I didn't have a lot of faith in Miss Ruby's follow-through—but the petition drive seemed to galvanize her. When my next shift came around, she offered me a ride again, and this time, along with her clipboard, she brought a stack of flyers for Dorothy's shop. "It's a great deal," she said. "You want one? You get a 10 percent discount on rhinestone work, and I get a commission for every flyer that gets turned in."

"I don't think so," I said. "Sparkly isn't really my style."

She looked at me with pity. "These shirts are the best quality, Nora—not like the cheesy ones from the center of town. Dorothy says they're odor resistant—you don't even have to wash them as much as a regular shirt." She twirled around slowly to show me. She had an undiscovered talent for sales, I thought, hoping Dorothy appreciated it.

Miss Ruby dropped me off and went to stand at her post by the store entrance. I had been behind the counter for about an hour, and a scrum of customers was bumping at one another's heels with the wheels of their shopping carts, when I heard Miss Ruby shouting, "Nora, Nora, Nora!"

I looked up from the slicer to see her running, or at least moving faster than I had ever seen her go, past the customer service alcove and through the bakery department. "Slow down!" I called. "Miss Ruby! Stop! You'll have a heart attack!"

"Nora, Nora, Nora!" she kept shouting. "It's Janelle!"

Now I was running.

"Hey, deli lady!" a customer yelled. "You can't just leave like that!"

"I got three hungry kids at home," another yelled at me as I rushed by. "You ought to be fired!"

Apparently unable to explain what was going on, Miss Ruby grabbed my hand and pulled me through the automatic doors and into the parking lot. I imagined Janelle collapsed, Janelle bleeding, Janelle gasping as her lips turned pale and her eyes rolled back into her head. I didn't know how to imagine Janelle—the Stop & Shop parking lot had never seemed like the setting for a disaster. "Over there!" Miss Ruby pointed. "She's chained herself to the buggy return!"

I stopped short. "What?" I said. "Why?"

Miss Ruby shrugged.

The spark of hope I had felt that Miss Ruby had mistaken someone else for Janelle—unlikely, given Provincetown's racial makeup—or that she had misinterpreted what she had seen flickered out when I got a closer look. It was definitely Janelle, sitting on the ground, her old Brooklyn-style bicycle chain wrapped around her waist and locked to the metal cage full of shopping carts.

She had bought us those bicycle chains shortly after we moved in together, after her bike had been stolen—the third one, she had said. "Good riddance," I had said, since it was the bike with which she had run into me, climbing the hill on Bradford Street—but then I reconsidered: if it hadn't been for the bike accident, we would never have met. So I had become proud of our bike chains, even a bit sentimental about them: Manufactured especially for use in the city, the links were supposedly forged of special hardened steel, fastened with a patented, cut- and pry-resistant U-lock. They weighed a ton and were hugely inconvenient to lug around on errands, and they were so intimidating I sometimes hesitated to take mine out; even coiled on the shelf it looked dangerous, like it would bite if I approached.

In Provincetown, where we assumed the thieves were less sophisticated, we had reverted to our old, flimsy cable locks—and now Janelle had found a new use for her Brooklyn chain. Next to herself she had propped a large sign:

NO MORE

hormone-treated meat
antibacterial cleaners
poisonous cosmetics
cigarettes

SAFE PRODUCTS NOW!

I sat down next to her. "Isn't this a little extreme?" I asked.

"Afraid for your job?" she said, clearly refraining from adding, "you sniveling coward!" That hadn't occurred to me—but it really would have been ridiculous to lose another position to Janelle's cause, especially since I hadn't stuck my neck out all that far, or even accomplished anything much. "Did they send you out here to try to sweet talk me?"

"Of course not," I said. "They know nothing about me and you. I thought you were hurt or something. Miss Ruby was in a terrible panic."

Janelle looked up at Miss Ruby balefully. "There's absolutely nothing wrong with me," she said. "Management refuses to meet with me, so I'm simply taking the logical next step. Just let them try to get rid of me now!"

A siren started wailing in the distance and grew gradually louder. "Whoa," said Miss Ruby. "Count me out of this." She handed me her clipboard and went off to get her scooter.

I was pleased to see that she had collected another page of signatures. I turned to Janelle. "Great, now the cops are coming. Honey, please, please unhook yourself so you don't get fined or arrested or something. That's the last thing you need; you should be taking it easy." I showed her the clipboard. "See? We're working on getting the insecticide spraying banned—that should help with the water."

"How would you know what I need?" said Janelle. "I'm staying right here; that's the whole point."

She was hyped up as I had never seen her before. I wondered if it was severe anxiety, which I could understand, or a misprescribed drug. In the evolution of her response to her disease, she seemed to have gone beyond anger to near-insanity.

A police car screeched into the parking lot, skidded in a half circle, and pulled up beside the cart return with a flourish. At the same time, a bicycle cop pedaled through the parking lot entrance, and the day manager, a big Cape Verdean woman who was usually quite benign and friendly, stalked out of the store. We were surrounded.

"Are you all here just for little ol' me?" said Janelle. Her obnoxiousness was new, too.

The officer from the car, a gray-haired veteran with an I've-seen-it-all expression, said, "All right, ladies, you're creating a disruption of business here. Time to move along."

Standing next to him, the bicycle cop nodded in agreement. "Just do like he says, and this won't go any further," he said.

I stood and brushed off my apron.

"Nora, go inside," said my manager. "Find a new apron, please; the lot is filthy."

"I was trying to help," I told her.

"Traitor!" Janelle hissed at me, doing nothing to unlock herself.

"This is your final warning!" the policeman from the car bellowed suddenly.

"Warn away," said Janelle. "I'm not leaving until these people agree to talk to me about all the horrible stuff they sell."

"How dare you say 'these people'!" said the manager. "We are doing our jobs! We are providing a service! Go to Orleans if you don't like our store."

"I will, eventually," said Janelle. "But I thought I'd start locally and branch out."

"You are being ridiculous, my girl," said the manager. "I wash my hands of this." She brushed her palms together several times and turned to go back inside. "Remove her quietly, please," she said to the policemen as she left.

The gray-haired officer rummaged around in the trunk of his car and pulled out a large hacksaw. "I'm sorry to have to do this, young lady," he said. "But I can't let this situation continue. Don't worry; I'll try not to hurt you." He began sawing at the chain around her waist as she watched.

"You're not going to get very far with that thing," she advised him.

After failing to make even a scratch on the link after several minutes of effort, he realized Janelle was right and turned to the bicycle cop. "Go down to the station and get me the bolt cutter."

"Also useless," Janelle pointed out.

"Let me try something, sir," said the bicycle cop. He knelt down beside Janelle and briefly examined the lock. Then he pulled a plastic stick pen from his pocket and with his thumbnail flipped the little stopper off the end. Working it into the lock's guaranteed-unpickable round keyhole, he twisted it, and suddenly, the mechanism popped open. The chain around Janelle's waist fell to the ground. "Wow," he said. "I saw this on the Internet but I didn't think it would actually work."

Janelle stood, brushed herself off, and started walking away. The policemen did nothing to stop her.

"Go on home," the older one yelled after her. "Sleep it off."

"That's disrespectful," I objected. "She knew exactly what she was doing. It was a legitimate direct action against something she sees as harmful."

Ignoring my words, he said, "Go on back to work, young lady." He looked at the bicycle cop and shrugged. "Just another day in P-town," he said.

"Yes, sir," said the bicycle cop.

The older one folded himself into the patrol car, slammed the door, rolled down the window, and leaned out. "Back to your beat, son. Nothing else to be done here."

I watched the cops leave, then rolled up Janelle's poster and gathered up the broken lock and chain. After putting it all away in my locker, I went back to finish my shift. The line was longer than ever. With my reappearance it began to advance, slowly, but everyone both in front of and behind the counter was exasperated with me for having caused the backup. Later, as I punched out, the manager gave me an official warning—but you had to accumulate three before they would even threaten to fire you, and the store was short-staffed just then. My job was pretty safe.

Roger Gets Over It

After Janelle's parking lot protest, it seemed to fall to me especially often to work the Saturday morning opening shift. "Nah, you just think so," insisted the manager when I objected. "You must take your turn like all the other girls. And look at me—I gotta be here all the time."

"But that's impossible!"

"Yeah, but you think I am, right?" She laughed. "My secret weapon."

Diligent and efficient, she did give the impression of omnipresence.

I'm a morning person, but not 5:00 in the morning, and the shift was misery, especially since I had to wake before dawn, usually after a night when Miss Ruby had had the TV tuned to the white noise and gray snow channel. She still kept to her irregular hours, despite Tony's attempts to nudge her into a normal human schedule of sleeping and waking. One early morning, when I emerged from the shower, she was bustling around the kitchen, frying me an egg.

"Thanks, Miss Ruby," I said, struggling with the egg. It was really very thoughtful of her.

She beamed. "No problem! I was up, so I thought I'd do something useful."

She must have been a fry cook at some point, because the egg wasn't bad, but all I felt capable of at that hour was coffee, black. Something with no nutrients.

And afterward, walking home, I was hungry and tired, and my feet ached from hours of standing. I had a headache, and I needed a nap. Passing the Green Teddy, I didn't feel up for a scene, played for the amusement of the patio regulars, with Roger, who came rushing out of the shop. I had been ambling along until then, but hoping he hadn't noticed me, I kept my eyes focused straight ahead and picked up my pace. Apparently, though, he had been watching for me. "Nora! Nora!" he called. "Wait up!"

"No!" I called back.

"I'm not going to yell at you!" he yelled.

I stopped. "Yell at me?" I said as he caught up. "Why on earth would you *yell at me*, since all I've been trying to do all along is help?"

"Not all along," he said. "You have to admit, I warned you."

"I have to admit? Come on, Roger, you of all people. You know how these things happen. It was supposed to be a minor flirtation, a fling."

"*Une aventure amoureuse.*"

"*Oui! Pas une affair de coeur. Mais, pourquoi nous parlons français?*"

"*Je ne sais pas,*" said Roger. "Your accent's terrible, by the way; I can barely understand you. I guess because it's easier than apologizing in English."

"I didn't deserve to be cut off, Roger. We were friends."

"Don't rub it in, my dear. It doesn't become you."

I let him take my arm. "What brought this on?"

"Don't know." He shrugged, and we walked in silence for a while. "Okay, I miss you. And I'm kind of worried about Janelle. Her moods—well, you know, you helped out with those cops the other day. She's so angry all the time—and she's normally so even tempered and basically happy. Which is so rare, and it's always been one of the things I love about her. Other people get blue—but not her. But now, when she's not berating me, she's hiding in her room."

"Really? That's awful; I had no idea. I thought you two were so close."

"We were. Are. But she says I get on her nerves. I drove her for a checkup the other day, to Hyannis, and she barely said a word the whole way there and back, and when I asked how it went, she literally snapped. 'Same's always.' She's gotten as monosyllabic as my *father*. I've been going to the library a lot."

"Wow, Roger, I'm so sorry. It's hard to even imagine all this; she's usually so kind hearted." I hesitated, because I was afraid to ask. "Do you think there's something else wrong? Something—you know—the doctor found and she hasn't told you about?"

"Oh, no, Nora honey, no. Don't even go there. It's a phase. Physically I really think she's okay. Tired sometimes, but she's actually coming back pretty well. Her hair's growing in and all."

"Well, who wouldn't feel that way?" I said. "Sad. Angry. The whole thing's depressing. Not that she should be venting it on you."

"She shouldn't," he agreed. "But then, who better to get mad at than some guy who's around all the time, bugging you to take a bunch of vitamin pills?"

"Yeah, she was like that with me, too, during her treatment," I reassured him. "But after a while she changed. She still loves you, Roger; I'm sure of it." When we reached the house, I had an impulse. "Come see my studio," I invited him.

"You have a studio?"

I pointed. "Up there. I needed a place to work, after Janelle put me out. Miss Ruby found it for me. I'm working on a big project; I'll show you."

We crossed the yard, and I fumbled with the padlock I had installed, although the wood was so soft that a perceptive thief would have realized he or she just had to give the doors a couple of good shoves and the screws would pull out. Finally the lock popped, and I let us in.

"Wow," said Roger.

Originally I had imagined somehow collaging images of P-towners and native animals into the backdrop of sea and sky and streets, but once I had started on the studies, I had become more interested in each individual—Baby and her long legs and her boots, Miss Ruby and the cat, which I had restored to her lap, unlike in real life. So now I was working on a series of large portraits, done in flat fields of color, with expressive faces and gestures, which I was very pleased about—I had been succeeding, I felt when I stood back and looked, at capturing the spirits of my subjects, something at which I had apparently not always been adept. "Skilled, certainly, but cold," my one reviewer had said. "Where is the energy? The risk? Is this portraiture in the age of the Internet?"

Blah blah blah, the Internet, I had thought at the time. It got blamed for so much I almost felt sorry for it. But the insult had planted itself in my brain as the definition of what I could and could not do—even as I understood how false and confining this was. For a long time my New Year's resolutions had included letting go of the idea that I couldn't portray emotion, along with all stifling labels and old resentments. But I hadn't ever totally succeeded, especially at the old resentments part, and yet now my supposed limitations had simply drifted off, as unnoticed and irrelevant as balloons after a party. In the Provincetown paintings I was onto something new.

"Roger, let me do you too," I said.

"You mean now? But I'm not ready. I just threw on this outfit, and my hair—I have an appointment to get it cut next week."

Roger was the sort of person who would probably look put together even after an all-night session in a back room with Blaze. And he didn't have enough hair to worry about. "You look fine," I said. "It's not a fashion shoot."

"Oh no, I couldn't. You don't understand how embarrassing—"

I patted the seat of the plastic chair and, as though I had hypnotized him, he sat down obediently. I set up my easel with the big pad of newsprint, rolled my shoulders back and forth a few times to loosen up, and took out a pencil. "Just a few sketches to start with. You can come back on a day when you've had a chance to get ready, and I'll fix the hair," I lied. I was pleased that I had thought of grabbing him unprepared, and I had no intention of fixing anything. Roger, in my opinion, had gotten handsomer as he had aged. His face had grown craggy, not wrinkled, so his smile, though friendly, was unexpected. And of course he kept himself in great shape. I supposed he had put on some weight as he had aged, just as I had, but it made him look less fragile, more grounded.

"Take out some of the gray."

"Sure, you'll look ten years younger when I get through with you. Maybe even fifteen." This was absurd, but Roger took it seriously.

"Well, okay, then, that would be great," he said. "Maybe you can do something about the abs, too. Tighten them up."

"Come on, Roger, I have my limits," I said, starting to sketch. "And don't guys like you as you are? Bears and all?"

"I am *not* a bear. I'm a clone."

"But no one's a clone anymore! How can you be a clone if there's no one to be a clone *of* ?"

"I just am," he said. "So what if I'm a throwback? The style always felt right to me. Plus, you wouldn't believe the amount of time and money it takes to get a pair of 501 Levis to fit right—all that washing and tailoring. They're an investment."

"So that's why you've always had a mustache?" I asked as I sketched it in. I had thought maybe he had a weak upper lip or an overbite that I had never seen. "Naturally it looks great on you!" I added, realizing he might think that my question was disapproving.

"For your information," said Roger, "I've never gotten any complaints about my upper lip. Or my lower one. And I have an excellent dentist. And as anyone but a lesbian would have noticed, the well-groomed but not overly mannered mustache is coming back as a male fashion accessory."

"Not those big twirly ones, I hope."

"Good goddess, no."

I tore off the sheet of newsprint I had been working on and started a new sketch.

"Actually," said Roger, "I like looking like a gay man of the 1980s. Even if no one gets it—I mean, the image isn't all that different from today. I'm not outlandish."

"Of course not!" I said.

"I am a memorial," Roger declared. It was an odd thing to say, and I stared at him. "You remember my boyfriend Paul Wong."

"No, I never met him. I only got to know you later, after—"

"Oh, right," he said. "And I'm so sorry about that, because it's a loss, for anyone who didn't have the chance to know him. He was so smart and quick and dear. Deeply, deeply funny—but never mean. I mean, *never*—completely devoid of that killer instinct most of us sissies have cultivated. For Paul it was all about delight. The human comedy. He was an enthusiast—just threw himself into whatever was happening around him. Totally in the moment, totally attentive, totally interested.

"He wasn't like you, though—not an artist. No gift for creating anything tangible or permanent."

"Just his life," I said, offering the cliché, in order to offer something.

"And that's over," he said. "Long enough ago that I've stopped glimpsing him on the subway, and I have friends like you, old friends, who never met him. I remember his face, his body, his voice, so clearly—but not anything specific that he said. Not his jokes, not even his favorite endearments. Isn't that strange?"

"So you wear his clothes?"

"Of course not, Nora—how grotesque! He was shorter than me!"

"I meant you adopted his style."

"At the time I was more the bohemian punk type—black, black, and black, right down to the boxers. Paul, though, in addition to the height issue, he was, well—*rotund*. I guess most people wouldn't have found him attractive, this chunky Asian guy trying to do the whole plaid-shirt-jeans-work-boots thing and mostly failing to bring it off. But somehow that made him even more sexy to me. Like a secret treasure. He'd come home, and his shirt would be half-untucked and his glasses on crooked, his hair hanging over his collar and falling in his eyes, but I never told him to get it cut more often. In bed I used to grab a handful, at the nape of his neck, and sometimes I just hung onto it all night.

"Sometimes I thought he should've had a stricter boyfriend, one who would have made him shave off the wispy mustache and put him on a diet. But Paul took such pleasure in food, in a dinner party—the shopping, the preparation. The tasting of the evening's concoction—he was always experimenting. The friends around the table. Toasting us and feeding us and charming us—he loved all of it.

"I want people to have a fleeting thought when they see me, subconscious almost: *I remember that; where'd they all go?* And then of course they'll realize."

"I wish I'd known him," I said. "I missed meeting a lot of great people."

"Yeah, too bad, right? Look," he said, closing his eyes for a moment, trying to find the patience to deal with my courtesy, "they're dead. Gone. I hate it when people try to pretend they're somehow still around. Remember that AIDS movie where all the dead guys came back at the end, onto the beach at Fire Island? I guess you weren't supposed to take it literally—the scene was about their friends remembering them or missing them. Whatever. They came back in good health, too. Buff, tan. No emaciated faggots hobbling around and throwing up and fainting, or disfigured, with KS blotches eating up their face."

Roger turned away and sneezed, or made some sort of choking sound, and when he turned back to me he was calmer. "I learned a lot of skills, though," he said, trying to sound upbeat. "There's that."

"What do you mean?"

"The Cherry Ames routine," he said. "And look at Janelle's new organizing thing. She's finally starting to understand politics—and I got schooled by the best, ACT UP. I'm trying not to take her outbursts personally." I glanced up from the easel to check the shape of a shadow, and Roger caught my eye. "You shouldn't either, Nora."

"It's a little more complicated between her and me, don't you think?" I said.

"Maybe," said Roger. "Maybe not."

Wet Suits

My reconstruction of events—and I've given this way too much thought: Baby and Broony emerge from the frigid Atlantic of late winter. Even wearing wet suits, they're chilled to the bone. But they're laughing, pleased with themselves as they peel off the suits, stripping down to their speedos and toweling off, and quickly pulling on sweats and fleeces. The swimming is something they've committed to doing, and they're proud of themselves, they're following through. They can feel their muscles getting stronger and their strokes more powerful. Their bodies have, after several weeks, become acclimated to exercising in the cold.

Baby pulls off her daisy bathing cap, shakes out her hair, massages her scalp with her fingers. Broony, too, tugs off her cap—plain black— revealing that she's cut off her braids. A true pro does not wear braids; she must be sleek all over like a seal. So she's gotten herself a crewcut, her only frill a strawberry-colored cowlick in front. Baby is entranced. She reaches out, rubs Broony's hair the wrong way, to feel its rough edge under her palm, and Broony shivers, not from the cold. Baby's hand moves to cup her chin as she leans in close for a long, warm kiss.

Oh, why go on! It was clear from the beginning that Baby would find additional interests—*additional*, not *other*. She had no intention of abandoning me. Baby loved everybody and would not hurt a fly. She was like a Buddhist monk on a road trip who, getting into the car, hesitates to flick on the windshield wipers to clear away the previous day's grime, for fear of harming any insects that might be clinging to the clouded glass. I had not, probably will never, attained her level of enlightenment, her compassion for all living, suffering beings, from bugs to Broony.

To me—I too was encompassed in the pleasure Baby took in each moment. But it wasn't enough for me: I longed for her undivided attention, which I mistakenly imagined I had had and lost to Broony. I became miserable and furious and clingy—not a combination that Baby found appealing or even, as most people would, guilt inducing. On my worst days, she tried to avoid me. I became convinced that she was screening her phone calls, although it's quite possible that she was simply busy in her store, enjoying a walk on the jetty—or swimming and frolicking with Broony. So I began avoiding her—to *show her*, to take my ridiculous revenge.

Of course, this is not how the world works. Throw a tantrum, and people have to pay attention. Withdraw, and no one frets about where you've hidden yourself or what she may have done to cause your disappearance; no one even notices that you haven't come around in a while—or if she does, it doesn't occur to her that it has anything to do with her behavior. I retreated into my studio, slammed the door, and waited for Baby to come crawling back.

The Ballad of Tony and Ruby

And waited. Sitting in the plastic chair with nothing to occupy my mind but jealousy and thwarted desire, which got boring after a while, I took another look at my mural. I left the backdrop I had made as it was and turned to the canvas I had started, in happier days, of Baby in her swimming gear. Then Tony volunteered to sit for me: I suspected she was looking forward to showing off her torso. "It's a point of pride with me, Nella," she explained, tugging off her T-shirt and wiggling around to find a comfortable position in the chair. She stretched her legs out in front of her and threw her arm around the back. "Some of the kids get a tattoo when they finish treatment—to show how their life is going to be different from now on. But the scars are enough for me."

"Nora," I said.

"Aw, come on," said Tony. "You know I'm just teasing you, Norm—Nora. Right?"

It was a concession, and I appreciated it. She had succeeded in nudging Miss Ruby into a better state of physical and mental health—which was more than I could claim to have done. "Right," I said. "Teeny."

"Ha!" said Tony. "You win. Teeny!"

I took out my pencil and began to sketch on the canvas. "How do you know Miss Ruby, anyhow?" I asked her. "I've always wondered."

"How does anybody know anybody around here?" said Tony.

"Oh, come on, Teeny," I said. Tony grinned. "You guys don't just know each other, you know, to say hi on the street."

"Long story," said Tony, turning her gaze toward the ceiling, where the past apparently resided, and shaking her head. "I don't know if I want to go into it."

"Sit still!" I said. "There's time."

Miss Ruby, Tony said, was different now from when they had first met. "The smokes, the family history—heart, her mom and dad both died young—it all kind of caught up with her at once. But twenty years ago, Rube was your true hellion. She had that black Iberian hair and the temperament to go with it, and she tore right through the lesbian community. She used to tend bar at the Pied Piper."

Tony became thoughtful, almost dreamy. "She had a suede vest she used to wear, with those short fringes, and she was *imposing*—never beautiful, not Ruby, but she had a kind of magnetism. The summer kids would come into the bar on Memorial Day, and she'd take her pick—a new one each season. You'd see them curled up together on the beach, parading up and down Commercial Street on Ruby's nights off. And when she was on, the girlfriend would sit at the bar mooning over her, and Ruby would be sending over all kinds of wacky drinks, full of cherries and pineapple spears and oranges and umbrellas, mostly juice really, with just enough booze so the girlfriend would be happy and loving come closing."

Tony shook her head. "Oh, man, those college kids didn't know what hit them, when Ruby took them up. They'd never experienced that kind of womanly attention, you know? There'd be a big scene at the end of August, when Ruby broke it to them that she wasn't going to write or call—crying and wailing and pitching the glassware. The old barflies used to look forward to it all year. But I'll tell you something. After it was all over they were goddamn *grateful*. Some of 'em still drop by. Ruby knew how to treat a girl.

"That all changed when I showed up. With me she'd met her match.

There were some who claimed it was perverted, two butches together. You know, they'd go like this when they saw us." She made two fists and bumped them together. Wrinkling her nose, she squeaked, "'But who leads when you dance?' We paid them no mind. No mind at all.

"I'd just been dumped out of the service," she continued.

"You were in the army?" I said, surprised.

"You would've thought that after spending all that time training me to be a medic they would've hung onto me a little longer. *That's* why I'm so good on all this health stuff, Nora. It's my specialty."

"So what went wrong?" I asked.

She looked at me in disbelief. "Are you naïve or what?" she said. She paused, sighed. "Like I was, I guess. There wasn't any 'don't ask, don't tell' then. Just 'don't don't, don't don't.' You couldn't tell me a thing, anyway. I was in *looove*. Like nobody else ever felt that way. My friends tried to warn me, but of course I didn't listen."

"Of course," I agreed.

Tony laughed. "Yeah, well. It was my girlfriend who ratted me out, can you believe it? Got herself into a snit one day, went to our CO. Said I wouldn't leave her alone, was trying to turn her gay." She paused. "I'll tell you something. That little so-and-so had turned a long time before I came on the scene.

"So I wasn't in the best frame of mind when I washed up here— even though I was excited about it all, couldn't wait to jump in. You know—P-town! Gay town! No officers, no rules. And Ruby and I were great for a while there, but then it all went south." Tony looked at me. "My fault."

"I didn't say anything," I said.

"No, but I could see you thinking," said Tony. "I agree. I admit to everything. My fault. I was drinking a lot, to excess, to be honest, brawling and carousing. I didn't remember the half of it; Ruby would tell me stories in the morning, and sometimes I would actually laugh at her, they were so unbelievable. Shoving people around. Taking over the dance floor and bellowing some song along with the DJ. Curling up in the corner and crying over my lost love, when I had Ruby, right there with her arms around me.

"What can I say?" said Tony. "You are looking at a genuine fool. One morning I wake up and Ruby's face is hanging over me like a big swollen moon. Two black eyes. 'Get out of here and never come back, you pig,' she says. I denied it up and down, but there she was, right in front of me. The evidence. I had a few bruises myself, but I couldn't believe how godawful she looked.

"I went way downhill after that. In the program they say you have to hit bottom, but I had to hit more than once, hard, bounce up and down a few times. Especially after the diagnosis. Ruby took me back for a while, because I was so sick and pathetic, and she's a good egg."

"She took me in too," I agreed.

"Look at the damn cats!" she exclaimed. "She can't stand to see them darting around the streets, all mangy! That's why we call her *Miss*!"

"*Miss* Ruby," I said, although Tony's explanation didn't make much sense.

"Right! Out of respect!" said Tony. "Even with her, though, I managed to wear out my welcome." She stopped.

I waited, but she didn't say anything more. Finally I asked, "So then what?"

"Then nothing," said Tony. "The end. They all lived unhappily ever after." She stood up and stretched, and came around to my side of the easel. "Let's see what you got."

"It's just a sketch. It's not finished."

"Do the scars in red," she advised me.

Signatures

Then suddenly everything was fine, and all the frustrations of life fizzled away like raindrops in the sun, because my Baby came back to me.

Well, to be honest, I went back to her. Sulking in my studio and working myself into a jealous frenzy just couldn't compare with spending a day with Baby, who lit up everything we did and made it an adventure, from having sex to picking up a few rolls of cash register tape at the hardware store for her shop.

I hadn't had to do anything dramatic. I went for a walk past Baby's store one afternoon after completing an early shift, and there she was, dusting the jewelry cases, humming along to the golden oldies radio station, occasionally bursting out with the backup, *oo just a little bit / mmm just a little bit / sock-it-to-me sock-it-to-me sock-it-to-me* . . . When I walked in, even before giving me an enthusiastic hug, she *tak-tok*-ed quickly to the door and turned the "open" sign to "closed."

A while later as we lay in her bed, Baby nuzzling my ear, her hand on my breast, she murmured, "I never left you, Nora." Her hand moved down to stroke my belly.

"But I felt like you did."

"But I didn't."

"No," I agreed. "Oh. Yes. There," I said.

I can't say it didn't hurt to think of her going, sometimes right after she and I had been together, to meet Broony, of all people. And I could no longer fool myself: There had been me; there was Broony; there would be others. Hadn't that been clear from the first moment she had

picked me up? Her frank flirtatiousness was what had attracted me—
and it was what would get me in the end.

"I have something for you," she said. "Something special." She
rolled away from me and reached over to her bedside table.

"Something from the store?" I guessed. "My ears aren't pierced, you
know. Maybe you could do them for me."

"No way," said Baby. "You think I haven't noticed your innocent
little earlobes? It's nothing like that." She handed me a packet, and I
tore it open. Inside were five pages of petitions, twenty signatures to a
page. Town meeting.

"You're incredible!" I said. "How did you get these?"

Baby wiggled her nose, like the witch used to do on the old TV
show, to perform her magic. The xylophone would play a little trill, and
I swear I heard it then. "I have my ways," she said.

I didn't ask any more questions—although I should have—and just
gave her a big hug and a smooch. My mind started racing. I would have
to write a proper anti-mosquito-spraying resolution and round up some
of the petition signers Baby had somehow materialized to speak up at
the meeting. And I needed to talk to Janelle, not through Roger and not
on the deli line. She was going to have to sit down calmly and listen to
me, so we could strategize. "Is there anything to eat?" I asked Baby. "Or
should we just go down to Spiritus?"

"Mmm," said Baby, pulling me toward her. "Just cuddle with me
for a minute, like a good little lesbian." Naturally, though, one thing
led to another, and we never did go out to Spiritus or anywhere else.
She grabbed and clung and clutched me to her, panting hard in my ear
like she was swimming the harbor, my hand up so deep inside her it
was like I held her beating heart. "Oh, you *sweet*," Baby murmured syn-
aesthetically. "Oh Nora, oh delicious."

I bet she doesn't talk to Broony like that, I thought.

Where Baby Comes From

The next morning I told Baby she owed me a favor, although that actually wasn't clear: She had gotten mixed up with Broony, but I had sulked and made myself scarce; she had welcomed me with open arms and loved me and given me petitions, and I? Well, I had made our breakfast coffee. "Sit for me?" I asked. "I'm getting a clearer idea of how my piece is going to work, and I want to draw you again." Really I had a perfectly fine sketch to work from, but I no longer wanted Baby to be wearing her swimming getup in my mural.

"Sure," said Baby. "Last time was fun—I love watching artists at work."

I noted the plural, then tried to put it out of my mind by bustling efficiently around the kitchen. "Okay, okay, great," I said, grabbing Baby's mug.

"Hey, I wasn't done with that," said Baby. "What's the rush all of a sudden?"

"Sorry. I'll go over to the studio and set up," I yelled over the water I was running in the sink. I washed and dried the mug, poured in the last dregs of coffee, and handed it back to her.

Baby took her coffee with lots of sugar and cream. "Cold," she said. "What's the point of a lovely slow breakfast if you're going to run off?" She reached over and took my hand. "Come back and sit down, sweet girl."

I kissed her cheek and extricated myself. "Meet me over there in an hour or so?" I said. I wanted to walk and clear my mind of plural artists and swimming competitions before sitting down at my easel.

I had barely gotten my pencils out when Baby showed up. "Let's do this," she said, settling into the chair and crossing her legs so her red cowboy boots were the first thing that struck you when you looked at her—or at least, that's how I drew her that day, with her long legs and boots as the focal point.

"I want to know about your name," I said, although I knew Baby liked to keep a certain air of mystery about her biography.

"I told you," said Baby. "I'll show you my birth certificate, if you want."

"No, but don't most parents have a name picked out?" I persisted. In fact, I didn't have a clue about most parents, as I and most of my friends had been just that much too old for the lesbian baby boom. Or too broke or too preoccupied with love or art or politics. It wasn't an option we had ever thought we would have.

"My name's fine," said Baby. "Just think of me as risen from the sea on a scallop shell. You know, without their influence."

"That bad?"

"Kind of." Baby nodded. "Pentecostals." They hadn't been at first. Baby's parents were the rebels of their families, zooming around the West Tennessee back roads in a rattletrap Ford, drinking cheap vodka. "They were always hoping to come across a still, where they could buy illegal moonshine," said Baby. "But there really wasn't much of that going on by then; it was more of a myth." They dropped out of high school, which no one particularly minded; the last straw came when Baby's mother forgot to take out her earrings and wash off her makeup before tottering home from a date one night. "My grandparents didn't hold with jewelry," said Baby. "You know. A woman's hair is her crowning glory, and she needs no other adornment." She ran her fingers through her own thick hair, resettled it on her shoulders, smiled at me.

I blew her a kiss. "Keep your face turned toward me," I said. "Like that."

"It was pretty predictable what happened after that," said Baby. "They shacked up together and kept on with the wild times until my ma got pregnant. But then after I was born, they repented. They wanted back into the fold. My ma in particular, she was so young, she wasn't going to be able to raise me without some help and advice. My grandpa baptized the whole family together. He was a minister, believed in total immersion.

"My pop, especially, got way drawn into the mystery and thrill of it. He was hot to start handling serpents."

"To *what*?"

"It's totally primitive; I can't even begin to explain it. In church they'll be singing and the minister will be sermonizing, and then some of the women start speaking in tongues and rolling on the floor, and the deacons bring in the snakes—they're in a big box, and they dump them out on the altar, and the men take them up. It's quite a thing to see."

Baby looked at me deadpan. "God protects them, Nora."

"He does?" I said. There had to be a scientific explanation, I thought. Does a pet snake recognize its keeper? Or more likely it was outright fraud: the snakes drained of venom or replaced with harmless ones before being produced in the sanctuary—something like that. I stepped back and squinted at my drawing on the easel, stepped forward again and began filling in the crosshatching on Baby's jeans, to convey the shape of her thighs.

"Of course not," said Baby. "They get bit all the time."

"People are nuts," I said.

"Well, they're crazy up here too, just not like that, mostly—one reason I love it," Baby agreed. "There was a big minister in the church who got snakebit and died. But they all decided it wasn't because he was a sinner or anything. God called him, you know? It was his time. My ma used to say she was rejoicing for him.

"We'd have to talk Pop down. Anybody could see from his life he'd never been particularly blessed, so we figured the snakes would just lead to another disaster. They raise them, you know, in these big aquariums in the living room. I've been in those houses; there's a weird smell, and every once in a while the snakes start twitching their tails and sticking out their tongues."

"Ick," I said.

"Oh, no, I was fascinated by them when I was a kid," said Baby. "The grown-ups were always shooing me away. It's funny, though—we were all deathly afraid of encountering rattlers and things in the woods. My ma had a fit if I wandered out of the backyard. Which I did all the time, or down the road.

"They could see where I was headed, I guess. On my fifteenth birthday they decided to drive out my demons."

Of course Baby would have demons. I sketched a little one with horns sticking out of its dyke crewcut, leering over Baby's shoulder.

"My parents invited a bunch of their church friends over to the house, and they all put their hands on my head and prayed over me. But my demons were very stubborn."

"I'd expect nothing less," I said, drawing a fat one clinging to Baby's ankle, with big breasts and hoop earrings and the wings of a gull. "But how could they tell?"

"Oh, who knows? They could see it in my eyes or something. My parents weren't bad people, Nora. They really believed they were doing good and raising me right, but from the beginning it was clear that I wasn't like them. It was like they'd hatched themselves a duck instead of a swan."

"A swan instead of a duck, you mean."

"Is that how that story goes?"

"Absolutely, sweetheart," I said. "The ducks can't see the beauty of the swan."

"My grandpa actually believed I was a changeling child—that the devil had switched me before he baptized us. He brought that story to my ma, the superstitious old goat! After, you know, my demons didn't leave. But she stuck up for me—she'd given birth to me, after all; she knew where I came from.

"All I knew was I could never live like them. I didn't have the faith. And husband, kids, garden, church? Hanging laundry and pulling weeds, day after day? Putting up the harvest in the fall? People up here think a garden's fun, but down there, it's survival. You ever listen to their hymns?"

"We don't sing a lot of hymns in Brooklyn," I said.

"Every single one of them is about how they're going to rest when they get to heaven. They had a hard life up there in the hills." Baby sighed. "You can guess what happened next."

"How could I possibly?" I said. What came after serpents and changelings?

"I ran off with my senior-year English teacher. A lovely woman. Or girl, I should say. She wasn't much older than I was, really, and we adored each other. She'd come down to help the poor and hungry."

"Your English teacher."

"I stopped thinking of her as that pretty quickly," said Baby. "It was so romantic, being desperate, on the run—although we weren't ever in any danger. Well, except from my grandparents, maybe. They thought Sally was the literal devil."

"Not your parents?" I asked.

"Not really. It was weird," said Baby. "My ma cried a lot, and so did I, but in the end she blessed me. 'You're a woman, Baby-Marie, and you'll make your own way in this world,' she said, and I've held that in my heart ever since.

"Sally and I banged around the country for a while—she had driven this old Chevy wagon down to us in Appalachia, so we had her wheels. And then one night in a bar in Cincinnati or some such godforsaken place, this ancient dyke in a leather cowboy hat with a turkey feather stuck in the band—I'll never forget her, Nora. Her face was as wrinkly as a prune, and she started telling Sally and me tales of *this* place, the sea and the light and the lesbians holding hands in the street. She was trying to sweet-talk us into coming home with her, but it was like she'd switched on a single light bulb over both our heads, and our minds were elsewhere.

So she got insulted and went off to get the bouncer, and he threw us out for being underage and for tormenting the regulars.

"We had to get a map to figure out even what state Provincetown was in. But that old gal was so right. Once I got here, I never wanted to leave. And I never have."

"Never?"

"Nope," said Baby. "Not if I can help it. I used to visit my folks on Christmas, but since they passed I just hunker down here all winter."

"What about Sally?"

"Living on lesbian land out in Oregon!" Baby said proudly.

"I didn't know that still existed."

"Oh, there's a few of the old communes hidden away in the woods. Sally couldn't take P-town. Too many people in the summer, not enough in the winter. Too much male energy—she said that was what started up her migraines. She and the girls out there went off the grid a while ago, and Sally's the one who figured out how to install the solar panels. She's great. When we were running around together she was a slip of a thing, with this long blonde hair that was always getting in the way when we kissed. Now she's a big-ass old butch with a gray crewcut. I have to write her actual letters, stick them in the mailbox. They don't believe in patriarchal computers."

"What about the patriarchal US postal service?" I said.

"They got themselves a woman letter carrier." Baby caught my eye, and we both started laughing. At the moment her story seemed hysterically funny: from the snakes and the demons to the mail lady and the lesbian communards. "I've found my place, my people," she told me, wiping tears from her eyes. "And how many can say that?"

False Pretenses

Miss Ruby stuck her head in the door. "What are you kids getting up to out here?" she asked. Since her health regimen had begun to have an effect, she no longer waited until events caught up with her to satisfy her curiosity.

"Miss Ruby!" said Baby. "Look at you, out and about! I'm confessing my sins."

"You'll never guess what Baby gave me," I said.

"You're right, I won't," said Miss Ruby. "I hate guessing." I handed her the sheaf of petitions, and she started flipping through them. "These are great," she said, surprised. "Look, here's Cha Cha Olivera—I forgot his name was Joseph. Theresa Cook, the old bat. How'd you get her interested in all the ecology stuff?"

"Oh, I didn't get into that," said Baby. "The old timers don't relate to it. I told them it was about raising the parking meter fees in the pier lot. Town decals exempted, of course."

"You've always been a smart one, Baby." Miss Ruby nodded approvingly. She turned to me. "Why didn't we think of that? Everybody likes sticking it to the tourists."

Baby said, "I told the gay guys it was to fly a rainbow flag over Town Hall."

"I can't believe this," I said. "Did you lie to everyone? Our petitions will be invalidated instantly!"

"No they won't, Nora!" said Baby. "Nobody ever reads anything. When it comes up at town meeting they'll just think they misremembered."

"I've seen it happen," Miss Ruby agreed.

"I don't think so." I shook my head, newly discouraged and annoyed at both of them. "I don't see how I can submit these signatures. They were obtained under totally false pretenses."

"You worry too much," said Baby. "Just try it."

She was right, to an extent. When I handed in the petitions at Town Hall, the clerk took them from me without suspicion, licked his index finger to turn the pages, and told me my item appeared to be in order and would be included on the STM warrant.

"The what?" I asked.

"Sit down, sit down." He waved at a chair next to his desk. "The special town meeting agenda. Haven't lived here long, have you? You haven't been in here before. I'd know. I remember everyone." A round, tan person with a bald head and shortish arms, he looked like a gingerbread man. He held out his hand for me to shake. "Chuck Pina. Pleased to meet you, Nora. Usually it's the same people, same signatories. Same issues too. And look, you've got some surprises here." He pointed at a scrawl on one of the pages I had handed him. "I never knew Cha Cha to set foot on dry land long enough to put pen to paper. Last I heard he was living on a houseboat he slapped together himself from junk he found on the beach. Moored it in the harbor. Good old Cha Cha!"

"He signed it Joseph," I pointed out.

"I know, I know, don't worry. It's all A-OK. You'll get your mosquito spray, or whatever you're trying for here."

"No, we don't want the spraying!" I explained.

"It's all in order," Chuck Pina reiterated. "Good luck to you."

The official Provincetown Charter starts with the words "We, the people . . . ," just like the US Constitution. Children in civics classes all over the country learn about direct democracy as still practiced in the New England town meeting, and the registered voters of Provincetown were proud to continue the tradition, although even they would quickly concede that it wasn't always the best way to make important decisions, with some attending just to speechify, some to disagree with every proposal, and some thoroughly baffled. Still, it was entertaining and a good opportunity to visit with the neighbors. The town moderator, chosen for her stentorian baritone and indifference to whether anyone liked her, ran the meetings, which mostly meant fielding amendments, and amendments to amendments, and banging her gavel furiously when the speakers flouted Robert's Rules of Order and wouldn't stop interrupting each other.

I, too, appreciated the democratic ideal as practiced in the town meeting, and if it sometimes got a little nutty, that was only appropriate for Provincetown. So leaving the building with a receipt for my falsified petition in hand, I felt like a turncoat, about to sabotage the people's vote.

The Special
Town Meeting

Janelle didn't feel good about the signatures either. I had taken a deep breath, called her number—which I knew by heart, of course, since I had once shared it—and with some difficulty persuaded her to meet me for coffee at the Green Teddy, nothing personal, just to discuss the next steps in the anticancer campaign.

We had had a stretch of freezing weather, so much so that temperatures in the forties felt almost balmy and the sun painfully bright. Squinting customers in coats and hats sat outside on the Teddy's patio, and Janelle and I grabbed a table. She was warily pleased that I had taken the initiative with the town meeting, but I felt I had to warn her about how Baby had gotten the petitions filled out, since despite the reassurances from her and Miss Ruby, it seemed inevitable to me, at least, that some people would feel exploited. Predictably, Janelle became furious. "Did I ask you to do this?" Janelle fumed. "Call this meeting? Thanks to you and that *person*, this is going to totally discredit my campaign."

I sighed. "Baby's on your side, Janelle. Just like I am!"

"I don't know you anymore," said Janelle. "Vandalism and now lies."

"Right, and who chained herself to the Stop & Shop?"

"That was civil disobedience, in case you've never heard of it! And the cops didn't even give me a warning. Anyway, I was feeling so pissed off that day, the action was very satisfying!"

"Oh, sorry, Dr. King!" I knew this was stepping over a line, but it felt so unfair that Janelle completely rejected all my efforts on her behalf. "So what you do is civil disobedience, but what I do is vandalism and lies?"

"I'm not having anything to do with it," said Janelle, standing up.

As she stalked down Commercial Street I could see Broony, who usually busied herself in the back when I came in, gloating at me from inside the store, but Bob bustled out with a complimentary latte. Pulling Green Teddy from his vest pocket, he danced him around on the table to cheer me up. "GT say, don't let it get you down," Bob said in a squeaky-toy voice. "He still love you."

"Thanks, Bob," I said. "I guess you're right. She's having a hard time."

"No, thank GT!" he squeaked insistently, holding the toy up to my face.

"Kiss, kiss," I said and pursed my lips. Sometimes Bob got a bit too literal about Green Teddy.

On the day of the meeting, sleet was blowing in horizontally off the bay, and I was half-hoping that too few people would show up to make a quorum, but no such luck. Tony gave Miss Ruby and me a ride, and I thought we would be the first to arrive, but quite a few old hands were already waiting in the cavernous foyer, stomping the slush off their boots, pulling off their hats, and hanging their dripping slickers on a wobbly coat rack. Town Hall was a historic and venerable building. The wide planks of its dark wood floor creaked loudly as the early birds wandered the room, greeting each other with a kiss or a handshake, and congratulating each other for braving the weather.

"Wouldn't send a dog out on a night like this!"

"Yeah, but how about an old fisherman? A little snow don't stop us."

"Us Portagees are made of the tough stuff."

The room grew humid and crowded, and people began filing upstairs to the auditorium. I was surprised at how many I recognized. Chuck Pina and an assortment of selectmen and other town worthies sat in the front, and right behind them, Reverend Patsy had grabbed a row for her congregants. My manager from the Stop & Shop waved at me, and sitting a few seats away from her was Margot in her leather miniskirt, although wearing wooly tights and big green wellingtons, as a concession to the storm.

Tony leaned over to instruct me. "These old queens," she said admiringly. "Nothing keeps 'em at home."

Baby had snuggled in beside me, and I was glad to see that Broony was sitting with Bob up in the balcony, not even within kiss-blowing distance.

"Where's Janelle?" asked Baby. "I mean, isn't this all about her?"

I shrugged. I hadn't told Baby about our latest argument. "The weather's kind of daunting. She's still recovering."

"Sorry, of course you're right," said Baby, squeezing my hand and crediting me, I could tell, with a measure of sympathy and tact that Janelle would have disagreed with her about. "I hope she can make it, though."

"Yeah, me too," I said, and although that was true, it felt hypocritical to say it.

The moderator had been banging her gavel for a while, and finally the noise in the room subsided, although it never really disappeared all evening. Most of the agenda was frankly boring, changes to budget lines and such. People looked around to see who was voting for which proposals, and stuck their hands up when their friends and allies did. Finally it was our turn.

"Resolved: that the Provincetown selectmen ask the Massachusetts Department of Public Health to rescind its plan for preventative mosquito spraying in our area," announced the moderator.

Rev. Patsy leaped up, along with her contingent. "Objection!" she called.

The moderator banged her gavel furiously. "Who do you think you are, Perry Mason?" she said. "Wait your turn!" She turned to me. "Ms. Nora Griffin! Tell us a little about your resolution."

I stood up. "We all know someone with breast cancer," I said, and I saw people around the auditorium nodding their heads. "Why should we introduce more harmful substances into our environment that will seep into our groundwater—which is already polluted enough? They don't even know if there will be a mosquito infestation this spring. And there's other stuff we can do to prevent that—getting rid of standing water, etcetera." I wasn't sure exactly what I meant by "etcetera," but I figured there must be other ways to prevent mosquitos from breeding.

Baby, Miss Ruby, and Tony burst into applause, and Patsy jumped up again. She pointed at the woman standing next to her, who was leaning on the chair in front of her. "This lady has Lyme disease," she said. "It's a terrible affliction. She can't work, she can barely stand up in this meeting to tell you her story herself, and we know exactly what caused her illness—while this supposed cancer-insecticide link is totally theoretical. Don't we as a community have a moral obligation to take action that will prevent suffering *right now*?"

Around us there was some confused murmuring. "But Reverend," a man called out. "All due respect, but you get the Lyme from tick bites. You all know I'd like to cull the damn deer—"

"Christ, there he goes again."

"He'd shoot anything that moves. The poor deer."

The man shouted over his critics, "—the girl here's talking about mosquitoes! Different bug altogether."

"All I can say is, keep your kitties inside. He'll be gunning for them!"

I heard the floor creak in the back of the auditorium and looked around. Janelle and Roger came in and sat in the back row, and Janelle raised her hand.

The moderator pointed at her, and Janelle stood up. "I have cancer," she said. "Or had. Who knows."

"But—" said Rev. Patsy.

"You had your say!" said the moderator. She turned to Janelle. "Go on, dear. I hope you're recovering well."

"I'm doing okay, thanks," Janelle told her, then continued. "I'm worried about the spraying, just like everyone else. But the people who signed the petition, they didn't know what it was all about. That troubles me too!"

Roger stood to support her. "Yes and on top of that—"

Irritated, the moderator interrupted him. "Wait a minute, young man, who are you? Are you a voter?"

"Not exactly, but—"

"Then sit down!" The moderator turned to address the audience. "Now, is this true? Are we all wasting our time here?" I squeezed Baby's hand, waiting for her subterfuge to be exposed, but no one spoke. A few people looked around and shrugged. "Okay, enough of this." The moderator banged her gavel. "I'm bringing this item to a vote. All in favor?"

Chuck Pina stood up and began counting, whispering the numbers to himself as hands popped up around the room, waving the cards that showed they were registered voters. There was a gap where Reverend Patsy and her people were sitting, but even without them it became clear that our motion would pass by a large majority.

Most of the voters didn't know or care about the insecticide spraying, but they hated it when some government agency tried to come in and tell them what to do—even when it was for their own good. They had been bickering with the National Seashore since its founding in 1961, although they were perfectly well aware that without the national park designation, their view of the sunset from Herring Cove Beach would have been obstructed by a block of condominiums, extending uninterrupted from the Sagamore Bridge to the traffic circle at the P-town Inn. I twisted in my seat to see what Janelle was doing, and my voter card floated to the floor. Her hand was in her lap. I bent over and scrabbled around to retrieve the card.

"Carried!" said the moderator. "The Provincetown selectmen shall request that the Massachusetts Department of Environmental Protection hold off on spraying this spring!" Baby, Miss Ruby, and Tony jumped up, pumping their fists and whooping. "What's this?" the moderator yelled. "No demonstrations!"

They sat down. Miss Ruby leaned over to me. "I can't believe we won!" she said. "I never win anything!" But I was less elated than I had expected; in fact, I was annoyed. *Of course you never win anything*, I wanted to tell her, *with these kinds of tactics*. Janelle herself, for whom I had done all the work, had spoken against it, and I myself had begun to doubt that forgoing insecticide spraying would do anything to prevent breast cancer. Uncomfortably, I wondered if Reverend Patsy and her parishioners had a point, about the immediate prevention of harm.

"That was great!" Baby said. "How come you didn't vote?"

"Of course I did!"

"I don't think you got counted. You were fidgeting around in your seat, and then it was all over."

I hadn't gotten my hand up in time. Janelle's abstention, of course, had been deliberate. People around the auditorium stood and began layering on sweaters and slickers and boots to venture back into the storm.

Outside, though, the wind had died down after pushing aside the clouds, and the sleet had stopped. I took Baby's arm in the bitter cold. "Look up, sweetheart," she said, pointing out the constellations. "Orion. The winter hunter."

Living in the city, I had never paid much attention to the sky, which stayed a kind of rosy color even at night, but in Provincetown, the pattern of bright stars seemed terribly close to us, and I thought, *That will go in my mural.* "I just hope we have a dry spring," I said. "To keep the bugs down."

All Other Boxes

When Reverend Patsy called to tell me I had to move my boxes out of her office, I assumed she was evicting them because of our disagreement over the mosquito spraying. "Not at all," she said. "Like the Christians say, turn the other cheek!" Quickly, she added, "Of course, we're not Christians, but we do believe Jesus was a great teacher.

"But my board doesn't like the clutter. The president came by the other day, and she had a fit. She says I have to learn to create a more professional impression."

For decades, on the church's signboard, below the title of the Sunday sermon and the posters for drag bingo, had appeared the motto *Everyone Welcome! Come as You Are.* "What about your signboard?" I asked Patsy. "Doesn't a little clutter make people feel more at home?"

"My board president says not if there's no place for them to sit. I really can't afford to get into any more trouble. You understand, Nora. The volunteers didn't do a great job cleaning up after our blessing of the animals, and the regular janitor was furious, I guess pretty reasonably, so I already got a big warning about that."

She was right, anyway. I couldn't leave my stuff with her indefinitely. The situation with the boxes was not as bad as it had been at first, since I had been plundering them for daily necessities, clothes and books and art supplies. I had been avoiding going through the rest of the contents, though; they were mostly remnants of my life with Janelle—vacation photos, birthday cards, a set of towels we had bought together that I had ended up with because after we had used them a few times she had condemned them as "too thick."

"How can a towel be too thick?" I had said. "Isn't that what's desirable in a towel?"

"These are like bathmats," she had said. "Thick and hard. Towels are supposed to be thick and fluffy. And they're an ugly color. Turquoise. What were we thinking?"

"I've been living without the stuff for this long," I told Patsy. "Maybe I should just toss it into the street on garbage day."

"Don't do that. The town won't pick it up! We'll get fined if you put those boxes out. You have to take them to the dump. And correctly sort all the recyclables, you know." She began enumerating categories: "Clear glass, green glass, beer bottles, water jugs. Coke bottles, Diet Coke bottles, daily newspapers, weekly newspapers. Oh, and Amazon boxes, all other boxes, soup cans, cat food cans, yogurt cups, and Styrofoam packing peanuts. Books—well, we don't recycle the books, they go on shelves for people to take home with them. Along with any bubble wrap—for the compulsive poppers. Everything else is trash."

"Wow, that sounds complicated."

"It's not so bad. There's bins for everything, and they're labeled pretty clearly. It just takes time. I've spent hours. But I don't mind; no one does. I run into congregation members and friends; we catch up. The dump is a true community space! I've often thought we should hold services right there. Ecology Sundays."

"I wonder what your board would think of that," I said.

"Ha!" Patsy burst out. "Don't ask! They are completely out of sympathy with creative spiritual expression."

"Are they giving you that hard a time?" I said. "I'm sorry to hear it; you certainly don't deserve it."

"No, no," she said. "Things will be fine. I was being ungenerous—one of my sins."

"Unitarians have sins?"

"Metaphorically. One of my flaws, okay?"

"Well, I don't think you're ungenerous," I said. "Look how much you put up with from me."

"You're very kind, Nora. But please don't repeat any of this. Everyone must find her own path, after all."

Mine was obstructed by boxes. I had suggested it facetiously, but thinking it over, I decided that throwing my stuff out wasn't a bad plan. There was simply no space for it in my current living arrangement. In my room at Miss Ruby's, I could barely turn around—"What do you need to turn around for?" Miss Ruby said. "Turn around in the living room!"—and in the shed, I needed the space for my paintings and my sitters.

Tony was up for any project that involved the use of her truck, so when my manager at work finally decided that I had done enough penance for Janelle's protest, and I got a Saturday morning off, I asked her to drive me to the church office. "Patsy will be so surprised when she comes in for Sunday services and the place is all cleaned up," I said.

Tony waited with the flashers on and the motor running while I hauled out a dozen boxes and loaded them into the truck bed. "I'd help, but if I get out, we'll get a ticket," she called as I trudged back and forth. "You know what they're like around here."

I thought I knew what she meant. The town expressed its ambivalence about tourism—needing the jobs yet resenting the invasion—through its parking regulations. During the summer, the meters were kept ticking away twenty-four hours a day, to squeeze out every possible quarter from visitors' pockets, and even during the off season the street signs were kept deliberately confusing, in the hope of catching the stray vacationer in a tow zone. "Don't you have a town sticker?" I asked.

"Yeah, but so what? I had a little fling with the meter maid—years ago now, but let's just say it didn't end well, and she still has it in for me."

"But that's unfair. You should fight tickets like that!" I said.

Tony just snorted.

At the entrance to the dump was a little shack, and Chuck Pina was sitting in the doorway. "Nora Griffin!" he exclaimed, jumping up and pumping my hand. "Congratulations, my friend! Great showing at the STM!"

"Special town meeting," Tony explained. "Guy knows everything—town meeting regs, recycling system."

"Thanks," I said. "It's nice to see you again. I thought you worked at Town Hall."

"Recording people's petitions is hardly a full-time job. Although sometimes there are so many of them, it almost seems like it could be. I do this on weekends." He turned to Tony. "There's a space over there." He gestured toward a surprisingly crowded parking area.

"It's always busy like this," Tony explained. "Scavengers."

I thought she meant the flock of bedraggled seagulls that was circling the dump, but when I cut open the first box, I found myself immediately surrounded by people. "Lemme see that," said one woman, peering over my shoulder. "Nice!" I had picked up a photo of me and Janelle, holding hands in front of our building in Brooklyn. I had asked a passerby to take it on the day I had moved in with her, and I had had it blown up to hang in our bedroom. "Can I have it?" she asked, gently tugging it from my hands.

"I guess so," I said, although it seemed odd that she would want a photo of a couple she didn't know—even though I thought we had looked especially attractive that day—the significance of which she couldn't possibly understand.

"What I really want is the frame," she explained. "I'll probably tear up the picture."

Oh, tear up my heart, I thought. It wasn't the first time that I wondered how I could have let things go this far. "Let me just take a last look."

"What, is that you? That skinny thing with the mop of black hair? Wouldn't have made the connection, you know? You were a baby! And the black outfits—were you guys coming from a funeral?"

"It's New York," I explained, letting go of the photo. The frame collector walked off with her find, and I berated myself, *No more Janelle-and-Nora. Clean out the remnants.*

The whole morning went like that. Every time I opened a box people bunched around me more closely. Chuck tried to shoo them away, and finally he picked up a box and carried it over to the row of recycling bins, the crowd trailing after him. Pulling out a clock radio, he began explaining to me how to figure out which bin to put it in: "It's plastic, so you might think it goes over there in number seven—but it's also battery operated, which trumps the plastic, so see, it has to go into that bin on the end. Fifteen." He started walking toward it, but a man cut him off and held out his hand. "I'll take that," he said. "What great stuff! I thought of skipping today; glad I didn't!"

"Watch, it'll all come back around," Chuck told me. "Once they get it home and try to figure out where to put it. People's houses are small around here. They don't have basements or garages."

"Exactly my problem!" I said.

"It's the same trash, week in and week out," he said mournfully.

When I opened a box of books, all hell broke loose. "*The Letters of Vincent van Gogh*!" exclaimed the frame lady, snatching the book and waving it over her head. "This is a treasure!"

"Wait a minute! Where'd you find that?" I said, grabbing it back from her. I didn't know how it could have appeared with my things. "I'll hang onto this one."

She glared at me. "You should've thought of that before!" she said. "Once you drop it off here, it's supposed to be fair game."

"Sorry," I said. "But I don't think a garbage dump has to be fair."

Chuck Pina nodded.

The Buddhists are right, I thought, to preach nonattachment to the material. It's so inevitably unimportant, unattainable, or ephemeral: a set of scratchy turquoise towels that neither individual would have bought on her own, the purchase of which could only have been made by the pair together, going for thickness and brightness and forgetting the fluffy factor. No couple, no towels.

I wondered if Chuck Pina could tell me where the bin was for that kind of thing.

The towels were gone, anyway, along with the rest of my things. Under Chuck's supervision, I broke down the cartons, tied them up with lengths of special biodegradable string that he provided, and piled them into All Other Boxes. I climbed into the truck cab with Tony, who had stayed inside, protected from the crowd and observing the whole procedure, and she drove me home.

Margot and Marcus

The storm on the day of the town meeting turned out to be the last Nor'easter of the season, and as warm, or at least warmish, days became more common, it seemed to me that Baby was spending more time than ever with Broony. Swimming, she said. I surprised myself by being somewhat less unhappy about this than I might have been. I had been getting it through my head that if I wanted to persist in my Baby entanglement, I would have to reconcile myself to her glad carpe-diem nature—but also, I was becoming preoccupied with my own project, even as Baby was with hers. My studio beckoned at all hours. And in the end, I thought, which of us would have more to show for it?

"It's temporary," Baby said, pulling me toward her one pretty April morning and covering my face with kisses before she ran off. She propped herself up on one elbow and, uncharacteristically, unpracticed at such a thing, attempted to reassure me. "Just until the Swim for Life is over. It's just a thing."

"A thing?"

"You know," said Baby. "Not like with you."

"Thing One and Thing Two," I said. I could almost see her demons, dancing on her shoulders. Lying in her bed, watching the sun silver-plate the wavelets on the bay, I remembered the freezing horizontal rain that the Cape also specialized in, and pulled the covers more tightly around us.

Baby laughed. "Oh hush," she murmured. "Don't move, don't think; let's just stay like this. You're my best thing."

After a while, my arm fell asleep. "Ouch," I said.

"Uh-oh, now I've really gotta run," said Baby, giving me a quick kiss on the cheek and throwing off the covers. Rummaging around in her dresser drawers, she produced her wet suit and yellow daisy bathing cap, stuffed them into a gym bag, and rushed out.

"I think you forgot your pink towel," I said, but she was gone.

After she left, I went directly to the studio. As I had been spending more and more time working on my mural, the place had gotten a little chaotic—not completely out of control but busy. I had filled a couple of big newsprint pads with drawings, and the sketches and paintings based on them, in various stages of completion, were hanging around the room, tacked to the exposed wall studs. With this work around me, I had evolved a process completely different from anything I had done before. Instead of focusing on one painting at a time, as I used to, I was doing all of it at once: pencil sketches, canvas priming, underpainting, blocking out of shadows and lights, filling in details. It was turning out to be helpful to be able to contemplate the ways the pieces complemented and interacted with each other—or didn't—and when I had had enough of one, I would work on another for a while. Before, I would have considered flitting around like that terribly undisciplined. When I had encountered a barrier, technical or imaginative, I had believed in slamming against it relentlessly until I busted through—not turning away or circumventing it. But pounding away day after day leaves you feeling bruised, not to mention demoralized, and I was learning instead to clear paths through the underbrush—around, under, up, and over.

As a result, pieces were falling into place. Miss Ruby and Tony had been among my first sitters, and I had hung the portraits of them, which I was still touching up, with the mural section that depicted, within the grid of Provincetown streets, an expanded close-up of one particular side street, and one particular dilapidated little house, a cross-section of which revealed Miss Ruby's recliner and some of her cats.

In addition to the people I had already painted, I wanted to include an image of Margot. In my mind, she had become representative of

Provincetown and its possibilities, even though I didn't know her at all, really, and I definitely hadn't always seen her that way. When I had first encountered her, singing in front of Town Hall next to her sign, "Living My Dream," which she would prop against the child's red wagon she used to drag her loudspeaker down Commercial Street, I had thought she was grotesque. Her long blonde wig, her leather miniskirt, her knockout gams and seventy-year-old face—the combination just seemed pathetic. Whatever her life had been before, had she really always been dreaming of this? A wig, a skirt, a pair of fishnet stockings, and a few songs made famous by that old capo Frank Sinatra? I averted my eyes from her performances. They embarrassed me—if not Margot, or anyone else for that matter: she always drew a crowd. The tourists would clap along.

After a while I got used to her. She was out in all weather—as intrepid as the gay motorcycle clubs (not the kind that own motorcycles) who march in sweltering late June LGBT pride parades, dressed hat-to-boots in black leather. I began to admire her grit and even her warbling. She didn't lip-sync or resort to falsetto but sang full-throated. Hers wasn't exactly a man's voice. Or a woman's. It was just—Margot's. I began to nod to her when I passed her on the street and to throw fifty cents or a dollar into her collection basket, on which a note explained that the change wasn't for her: after a lifetime of employment in the finance industry, it reassured her listeners, she was quite secure and enjoyed being able to donate the money to the Provincetown animal shelter. Margot was a lover of strays.

And then of course she had signed my town meeting petition—one of the few people who had done so fully understanding what it was for. I caught up with her one day as she was packing up after her last song and asked if I could paint her portrait.

"Who could say no to that invitation?" said Margot. "Would you like me to pose like this"—she planted her feet and flung her arms open wide—"or in my street clothes?"

"I thought those were your street clothes," I said.

"Oh, come on, sweetheart, you've seen me a million times in front of that fish counter in the Stop & Shop."

"Deli," I said, embarrassed that I had no idea what she was talking about. As far as I knew I had never seen Margot anywhere but in front of Town Hall, doing her act. "Can I try you both ways?" I asked.

"Why, I'm all aflutter!" Margot put a hand to her chest and wiggled her fingers. "No one's asked me *that* for a dog's age!" She smiled at me, and suddenly I could see the older gentleman I had waited on a few times. With his white hair combed back from a receding widow's peak, big translucent ears, and gray cardigan sweater, he looked European, or somehow not of this century—although not of a past one, either. He always left a tip, not common practice. "I'll bring along a change of costume. When and where shall we meet?"

I told Margot how to find my studio, and we made a date. I wasn't sure who to expect, my customer or Margot. As I waited, I flipped through my newly rescued copy of the *Letters of Vincent van Gogh*, realizing sadly that the book didn't have its old charisma, from when I was in college. Perhaps I had learned too much: I couldn't take seriously Vincent's constant pronouncements about art and, especially, love, knowing that in his life, he couldn't get along with anyone—as much as he longed to—much less love them.

When I opened the door, there was my customer, dragging a small tangerine-colored suitcase on wheels. I was disappointed: a drag queen would have been a more interesting subject, I thought; the man before me in his street clothes was not nearly as colorful. In fact, he looked quite gray.

"It's Marcus," he introduced himself. "I felt ever-so-mildly *fatigué* this morning, and it's restful, on occasion, not to have to encounter one's fans on the street, don't you think? It happens, at my age. But I can change if you'd rather." He indicated the suitcase.

"Let's start this way," I said. "Since this is how you're feeling. Is that how it works? That you choose every morning when you wake up?"

"My goodness, no," said Marcus, lowering himself onto the plastic chair. "That *would* be trying. There's usually no choice necessary if I'm not going out. I have a few lovely at-home kimonos, which are also suitable for receiving the occasional special guest. Of course, there are times when loungewear just won't do, you know, such as for work in the garden or kitchen or making simple repairs. For those tasks I have a very practical coverall. Not elegant, you understand, but practical, such as a mechanic or perhaps one of our Cape Cod fishermen might wear. The Marine Supply emporium carries a variety of butch colors—khaki, gray, a kind of blue herringbone affair.

"If I'm going out, though, unless I'm in a great rush, or as today, feeling a bit under the weather, Margot emerges."

I had begun sketching, but Marcus's ears were giving me problems, overdominating the picture. Oddly, I had never noticed anything unusual about Margot's ears; maybe they were flattened by the wig. "Turn your head just a little toward me," I said. "Do you mean that you're not quite in control of Margot?"

"No, I wouldn't say that. I suppose it's more that I invite her to appear. She is such a delightful . . . manifestation. I feel truly fortunate to have discovered her. Dis-covered, if you see what I mean. I'm not sure how to describe it to you. Or anyone, really." Marcus sighed, then continued. "The queens in this town don't seem to understand what I'm talking about. They consciously invent their personae—the name of their first pet, plus the name of the street they lived on when they were eight, that sort of thing. Whereas Margot, she—well, she just is. Naturally and organically."

"Organic drag," I said.

"Exactly," said Marcus. He seemed pleased with the idea. "You could call it that."

"When did Margot first—emerge?" I asked him. This was what I had really wanted to know. The origin of his unusual dream.

"Oh, my dear, Margot's always been with me. Always. I mean, she may have changed her style a bit, to keep up with the times, you know. But she is who she is and always has been, since I can remember. Singing and making people happy.

"Most people. Not my parents, of course. Although it's from them I got my love of Frank Sinatra—so ironic. Old Blue Eyes, my mother called him, the star of her youth. She and my father were so young when they had me, married right out of high school, you know. She was one of those girls who would scream for him, like we did for the Beatles—do you remember, my dear? It was such fun."

"Actually that was before my time," I said. "I wasn't born until 1976."

Marcus looked taken aback, as though this was an impossibility. "Well. I think my mother had a little *pash* for him all her life," he continued. "My dad had blue eyes, and as a small child I used to wonder, Is that why she married him? Certainly it wasn't because he was such delightful company. Going to work, coming home. The Organization Man, they used to call it. Tennis on the weekends.

"He tried to teach me once, his little sissy. On those unshaded courts, a machine hurling the balls at you, one after another. A literal *cannonade*. With the sun beating down and that rubbery asphalt smell. 'Look smart!' he kept shouting. 'Don't lock those knees!' Finally I just fainted dead on the ground.

"I panicked when I opened my eyes. He was standing above me, and I had the terrible thought that he was going to abuse me somehow. Slap me. Call me names. I don't know why that occurred to me; he'd never done anything like it before. And he wasn't a bad man, just hopelessly conventional—probably also a little what we would now call OCD. Obsessive. I'm quite sure it never entered his mind to lay hands on me then or any other time. No. He helped me up and got me some water and apologized for taking me out on such a beastly day. And you'll never guess what he told my mother about the whole thing."

"Was he disappointed?"

"Not at all!" said Marcus. "He said, 'Our Marky has other talents.' Who knew he had it in him? Such kindness and insight. I'm convinced he must have had hidden depths, although I don't think he even *hinted* at any such thing ever again, to me or to my mother."

"So is that when you started wanting to live your dream?"

"Perhaps so, my dear, perhaps so. I had a long way to go between that charming moment and this one, but I do believe my father would give my work here his blessing. My late mother too—because Margot's always shared her love for Old Blue Eyes, you know."

Marcus stood and stretched his arms up above his head, then out to the sides, twisting to the right and left a few times, and finishing by flopping over to touch his toes. "I think we've done enough for today," he said. "I'm simply *pooped*."

"Thank you for doing this, Marcus," I said, superpolite, trying to match his elegant manner. "I really enjoyed it; I hope you did too."

"A pleasure," he agreed.

"But do you think Margot would be willing to come over one day and let me draw her, too?"

"Why don't we leave things as they are," said Marcus, coming over to my side of the easel to examine my sketches. Showing these always made me uncomfortable—they were basically notes, some quite detailed but others just a few lines or shadings, useful to me, but probably indecipherable to anyone else. They could cause the sitters a pang of regret or even anger, as they wondered whether this was all they added up to: a pattern of lines and shadows. But Marcus nodded. "A work of art should express both the inner and the outer truth—don't you agree?"

After he left, I picked up my book again. "Do not quench your inspiration and your imagination," I read. "Do not become the slave of your model." On a new sheet of newsprint I drew the chair, Margot's wig draped over the back of it, her skirt and stockings folded and stacked neatly on the seat.

Triangles and Squares

Since Roger and I had reconciled, he had sat for me in the studio a few more times, and then we had gotten into the habit of meeting for coffee on the Teddy patio when I had a free morning. We would chat about this and that—he had become especially interested in the progress of my artwork, or more specifically, of my portrait of him—but our conversation would inevitably settle on Janelle: her recovery, with its ups and downs; her ever-lengthening walks along the seashore, especially during her downs; her new clients; her dates.

She had begun dating. I was hardly in a position to object, but underneath everything that had happened, and even with Baby and my masterpiece to keep me busy, I missed her. I didn't want her to leave me behind, as she found happiness with Carmen or Nancy or most often these days, most ominously, the formidable Mi'Kay. Fellow techie and tinkerer, fellow walker on the beach. Unlike the others, whom Janelle had met over the Internet, Mi'Kay had apparently dropped in on Janelle's survivor support group at the Outer Cape clinic.

"Tall, dark, and handsome," said Roger.

Even he was taken with her.

"And Mi'Kay's been so good for her," he babbled. "She has this unique warmth, which I guess you don't expect from someone that beautiful—those incredible cheekbones—and she's so patient, when even I am ready to throw up my hands. Mi'Kay always seems to know just what to say, or *do*, you know, when talking just isn't what Janelle needs."

"So I guess not much of an intellect."

"Are you serious?" He looked at me. "She's a professor at MIT. On sabbatical this year—that's why she's spending so much time down here. She's renting a little cabin out in the East End, finishing a book. She's actually very busy with it; her publisher wants it as soon as possible, because it's going to blow her field wide open. I don't understand the whole thing, but it's something to do with global warming, and how to turn it around. They're already booking her onto *Today* and all that. And yet, Mi'Kay's so down to earth, I bet even you would love her."

"Mi'Kay, Mi'Kay, Mi'Kay," I said. "You sound very impressed."

"Who wouldn't be?" he said. "Don't tell me you're jealous."

Of course I was. And in the worst way: I didn't exactly want Janelle back, which was clearly impossible, but apparently I didn't want anyone else to have her, either. Especially not someone as all-around wonderful as Mi'Kay. "Oh, uh-uh," I said, trying to sound casual, and not trusting myself to say actual words. Janelle would have said I had no right to feel the lump in my throat.

In fact, she only barely missed the opportunity. "Okay, I'm here," she said, standing over our table.

Roger jumped up and hugged her. "You're so brave, sweetheart!" he said.

Janelle glared at me over his shoulder. "Roger begged me to do this," she explained. "To come by when you'd be here."

"Nora appreciates it," Roger prompted me.

"I do," I realized. "Roger says you're dating other people—"

"These days just Mi'Kay," said Janelle.

It was worse than I had thought. They must have had the Talk and decided on monogamy. "Right," I said. "Roger told me about her. She sounds great, Janelle, really. I'm happy for you."

"How come your face is all blotchy, then?" she said. "Or am I just not used to looking at a white girl all the time anymore?"

"Oh, come on, Janelle," said Roger. He took her hand and mine and tried to put them together. "Kiss and make up."

I could actually see her thought: *You've got to be kidding.*

"I miss you," I said. "I don't want us to . . ." For a moment I couldn't go on, and I guess my face got even more blotchy. "I don't want us to go on like this, avoiding each other and being mad. I don't want to lose you forever," I said in a rush.

She sighed. "These past few months . . . Look, I know you're trying. With the posters, and the town meeting. I know you did those things for me. But you never get it right, you know? You didn't used to be like that—did you? Your hot affair, your painting or whatever, that Roger's always going on about. Good for you for getting back into your art instead of those tacky earrings—"

"—They weren't tacky! I liked them!"

"—but squatting in some guy's toolshed? You've become so unpredictable!"

"Janelle," I said. "Remember last summer, when you told me I was having a midlife crisis? I didn't agree, but you were right. I was stuck. *We* were stuck. And since we moved here, I guess I've started coming unstuck. Haven't you changed too? Look at the action you did at the Stop & Shop. You never used to get so carried away."

"Maybe not on the outside. Maybe you just didn't see it. Maybe that's the problem. Mi'Kay gets me; maybe it's a black thing."

"Oh," I said. The great unspoken. Of course, we had talked about our racial difference a lot at the beginning, in those long, irresistible pre- and postsex conversations one has, when her stories haven't yet become familiar but are full of exciting revelation, and even yours, as she listens, seem to acquire new significance—but after a while, as we had settled into a day-to-day life with each other, we had neglected that particular discussion, and at a certain point I, at least, had told myself that was okay. That all the things we had in common, like gender and sexuality and class and age and even New York geography, transcended it. Janelle, I now realized, had never exactly voiced her agreement; if I alluded to my idea she had just nodded: *Umm hmm.* "I don't know," I said. "I thought we understood each other pretty well."

"I thought we did too," she conceded. "But look at what happened! So maybe not. And I don't think it's so great for me to just let my feelings shine out, any which way. When I think about that day, I'm embarrassed.

So I expressed my anger, so what? The Stop & Shop people won't even let me in the store now, much less meet with me and reconsider selling some of their noxious products." She paused. "And people like me will just keep getting sick."

"Honey, don't—"

"I thought I was finally getting through everything, coming out the other side, returning to normal, and now you want back in my life? As my friend?"

"I do," I said. She was about to turn away when Broony rushed out onto the patio.

"Aha!" she said, pointing at me and Janelle. "You were not expecting me! But I am here, and I catch you flirting with your woman. I will certainly tell Baby!"

"Hey, what's your problem?" said Janelle, grabbing my hand as Roger had tried to make her do and giving it a squeeze.

"Like Baby would care," I told Broony. "Baby knows all about Janelle."

"Yeah," said Janelle. "We're all old pals. So leave us alone. I don't know what business our conversation is of yours."

"Bah!" said Broony. "Think what you want!" She turned away and went back into the store.

"Nice friends you have," said Roger.

Janelle extricated her hand from mine. "What was that all about?" she asked.

"Broony," I explained. "Brunhilde. She works here, and she and Baby go swimming together. They're having a thing."

"A thing," said Janelle.

"A thing," I said.

Janelle caught Roger's eye and gave a short, snorting laugh.

"Swimming," said Roger. "Is that what you deeks call it?"

Janelle turned to him. "Mi'Kay had to go into Boston for the day to meet with her agent, but she should be back by now, so I'll be over at her place. You have my key, right?"

"No problem," he said. "Have fun."

"Kiss kiss," she told him. Then she leaned down and gave me an awkward sort of hug around the shoulders. "I don't want you to disappear from my life either," she admitted. "I think that's why I keep harassing you." Then she rushed off.

"That," I said, "I didn't expect."

Roger watched her go and then leaned over to me confidentially. "I think she's finally put back on a few pounds. Mi'Kay is such a good cook."

"Naturally," I said. "I mean, I'd expect nothing less."

He looked at me. "Sorry," he said. "I get carried away."

"I'm trying, you know?" I said. "But enough already about Ms. Perfect. Or should I say doctor. Dr. Perfect."

"Okay, blotchy-face," he said.

It was my turn to give a short, snorting laugh. "I never realized I blushed like that."

"The things we don't know about ourselves," said Roger. "Let's go."

He left for Janelle's, and I walked across the street to the town beach. The spring sun was making an effort, but the sand, when I sat down, was cold. The tide was so far out, exposing sandbars and patches of bright green seaweed nearly all the way to Long Point, that you could have walked rather than swum there—and indeed here and there in the distance small, silhouetted figures were making the trek, the occasional dog leaping beside them. The sailboats and dinghies that usually floated near the shore had been left high and dry, their anchor lines as crossed and tangled as my thoughts.

Janelle-Nora-Baby, Nora-Baby-Broony—a triangle is easily thrown off balance, like a three-legged table. But Broony was, Baby had hinted, on her way out, and now Mi'Kay had arrived, and our wobbly triangles seemed about to open into a square: Nora and Baby, Janelle and Mi'Kay, each in her corner. The boat was no longer rockable. Instability, though, creates movement, and there's a reason hip folk call couples *squares*.

The Call

Miss Ruby was leaning to one side in her chair and snoring when I walked in the door after a shift, with a cat in her lap and the television cackling. "There you are!" she murmured. "I was hoping you'd be back soon."

"No you weren't," I pointed out. "You were sleeping."

"Was not," she said, sitting up. "I came back from walking with Tony, and I was thinking." Her eyes fluttered closed. "You made us some signs, and we were dancing—"

I put my hand on her shoulder and shook her. "Wake up!"

She reached up and patted my hand. "Maybe that *was* a little dream. About the Swim," she said.

"I still don't know what you're talking about."

"One of those ideas of Tony's. I mean, the harbor's pretty clean early in the year like this, but you just know they'll be closing beaches once the season starts, and the town gets crowded. Stresses the septic systems."

"That's disgusting!" I said. "Are you serious?"

"It's the goddess's truth. So Tony says if you paint us some signs about the pollution, then when the people are coming in from the swim, we could hold them up." She brushed the cat off her thighs purposefully, as though she meant to get up and walk a picket line right then, but it immediately jumped back into her lap. "Ye-es puss-puss," she said, stroking it, then looked up at me. "I mean, isn't that how we got started on all this—the water?"

"I guess so. It seems like such a long time ago. But isn't the Swim supposed to be festive? Not," I admitted, "that I'm looking forward to it."

147

"Everyone goes," said Miss Ruby. "You'll see—it's fun."

"Cheering on Baby and Broony. What's fun about that?"

"Well, if you make us some signs you'll have your own private reason to go," said Miss Ruby reasonably.

So I walked over to the hardware store to get a few big sheets of ocean-blue oak tag paper and superwide markers in several colors. On the way back, I thought about designs. The posters would be dual purpose. Innocuous on one side, like the ones a lot of the spectators would be carrying, they would read "Go Baby!" (even for the big day, I refused to root for Broony). But then we would reverse them as the swimmers splashed into the finish line, and the other side would ask something like "What's in the water?" A bit cryptic, but since we had already done one action using questions like that, I hoped people would get it.

Picturing how I would decorate the posters around the edges with hieroglyphics of waves, birds, and sea creatures, I nearly crashed into Reverend Patsy as I passed the church. She was pacing carefully in front of it, as though the uneven bricks of Commercial Street were a tightrope. "Good lord!" She looked up, startled. "Nora! I didn't see you. My walking meditation. And you seem lost in thought too. A penny for them!"

I didn't want to tell her about our plan for a protest at the Swim and risk getting into another argument—her reactions were so unpredictable. On the one hand, she might want to join in, but on the other she might decide we would be violating the spirit of the day, or something. "Just thinking about my mural."

She fell into step beside me. "A mural!" she said. "I didn't know. How creative! What's it for?"

"It's not really *for* anything."

"Ah, the age-old question," said Patsy. "Must art serve a purpose?"

I shrugged, playing the inarticulate painter. Debating the purposes of art was something I hadn't done since college days. I used to enjoy those sorts of passionate, after-dinner sessions, and they certainly helped me when I had to get in front of a classroom, but I had discovered it was a relief not to have to be so constantly analytical. "I don't know; this piece is just something I started doing. I'm still not sure what it will look like in the end, but lately I've been working on portraits of various Provincetown people who I've met," I said. "Miss Ruby, Baby, Tony. Margot. Roger."

"Roger? Who's Roger?"

"An old friend," I said. "He's been spending a lot of time here, helping Janelle."

"Still, I don't see why he belongs in it."

"Patsy," I said, feeling annoyed. As a minister, she couldn't seem to stop herself from advising. "It's my mural, and he's my friend. So, he's in it."

"What about me, then?" she said. "I'm your friend too."

"And I've been meaning to ask you!" I said, exaggerating a little. She was right; she belonged in my piece—but for some reason I had put off talking to her about it. Today, for her meditation she was wearing, as always, her collar—which would be a nice touch in a portrait—with a blaze-orange windbreaker against the spring chill and a pair of faded red sweatpants with the word P-TOWN in big letters across the butt.

She noticed me evaluating her outfit. "A gift from our teen chat circle," she explained, about the sweatpants. "Not the most clerical, I suppose, but my meditation teacher says to make sure to wear something loose and comfortable."

"Let's do it," I said. "You look great." I could make posters another time, I thought, and she was wearing the perfect Reverend Patsy getup.

"Now?" she said. "But what about my walking meditation? And I grabbed this jacket from the free box; I really should put it back."

"I'll disguise it," I said. "Seize the time!"

"I see," she said. "Spontaneity! Well, I was almost done anyway, and you broke my concentration."

"And we're almost at my studio."

"It was meant to be, then," she said cheerily. After we arrived, as she was settling into the plastic chair, she continued, "Although maybe I shouldn't say that. It's just coincidence that I ran into you. Or really, you ran into me."

Setting up my pads and pencils, I wasn't really listening.

"And some people say there's no such thing," said Patsy. "Fate, destiny. Versus free will. What do you think?"

"Absolutely," I said. "Free will. Try to relax more and not grip the chair arms."

She glanced at her hands and quickly pulled them back from the chair, settling them onto her thighs, palms up. Then she rolled her head a few times from side to side, looked up at the ceiling, and exhaled noisily, sticking out her tongue. Looking back down and closing her eyes, she asked, "Better? It's my meditation preparation. Very effective. I've done it enough by now so it almost automatically puts me into an alpha state . . ." Her voice trailed off.

"Can you do it again? I just want to get that part where you stick out your tongue."

Patsy opened her eyes. "It's not a performance, Nora. It's part of my spiritual discipline. I was thinking of our session here as a kind of co-creative, co-meditation. But perhaps for you, the iconoclastic artist, it's something different."

"I'm sorry," I said. "It looked interesting, that's all."

"Honestly, I wonder about the visual arts sometimes. All the attention you people pay to appearances." She stopped, then said, "Wow. That would make a good sermon topic."

"In this town?" I objected. "Aren't most of your congregation artists?" I was hardly the only person in Provincetown with a day job and an art habit; sometimes it seemed like every person you met was busy creating in their spare time: The guy who ran the taffy store painting quite good watercolors of the ever-changing view of sea and sky from the back of his shop. My manager at the Stop & Shop piecing quilts—the kind you hang on the wall, not the kind you sleep under—who had been sewing frantically for months to get ready for an exhibit she had lined up in Boston in July. The teetotaling dyke who drove for Art's Dune Tours, whose photographic specialty was tourists' tattoos—she had become so expert at it that she had begun a second job at the tattoo parlor, providing her services to the grateful clients, because isn't the whole point of getting a tattoo showing it off? Her own skin she had preserved unmarked—she hadn't permitted even the most conventional piercing in her ears—and on the hottest days of summer, when she arrived at the shop wearing running shorts and last year's Swim T-shirt with the sleeves cut off, the tattooer would look greedily at her hefty, pink arms and legs. Too bad; she had an ineradicable fear of needles.

People always said it was the light, and the way the surrounding ocean glittered with it, then bounced it back to shore, that inspired the artistic outpouring, but I wondered if it wasn't also the prospect of the long, lonely drag of winter after the frantic festivity of the season that drove people to their various canvases.

"Oh, you're probably right—I'd be stepping on too many toes," said Patsy. "The board chair says I have to learn to respect people's choices—and of course I agree with that. Though sometimes, you know, it feels like cowardice."

"But what do you have against beauty?" I asked her.

"The Muslims and the Jews forbid the representation of the human form, did you know that? They believe it's against their commandments—graven images, and all that. They think it gets too close to idolatry."

"Harsh." I put down my pencil.

Patsy got a distressed look on her face. "There, you see? I've done it again. Ruined things. Stepped in it! That's what my meditation teacher calls it. The walking was supposed to help. Please, finish your drawing." She went through her stretching routine, ending up again with her hands on her thighs and her eyes closed.

I tore off the page I had been sketching on and stared at the new one. "It's not working, having you just sit in the chair. Let's try something else." Patsy's philosophical dilemmas were making me feel claustrophobic. "Let's go outside."

She blinked a few times and obediently, for once, stood and followed me out the door.

"Try standing next to that bush," I suggested, although as soon as I said it, I realized the scene was probably a mistake. Unlike other bushes in the yard, which had started to put out red shoots and tiny buds, the one by my studio door was still a heap of gray sticks.

"Like this?" Patsy planted herself where I had indicated and clasped her hands behind her back. Then she clasped them in front, then crossed her arms across her chest. She hooked her thumbs in the waistband of her sweatpants but quickly removed them. "I don't know what to do with my hands!" she said, holding them out to me, as though I could take them and do something with them.

"I don't know either," I said. "Can't you just stand naturally?"

"Oh, for goddess's sake!" she said. "What's *natural*?"

At that, we both started laughing. Janelle, my scientist, had been a stickler about that. "*Ridiculous*," she would say when she heard of some preacher damning our kind because of our unnatural lifestyle. "*As though human beings aren't thoroughly socialized creatures.*" I told Patsy, "Stand queerly, then."

"Ha! Nice," she said. "But I don't think this is working out."

"No, don't say that. Sometimes it just takes a while to loosen up. Forget I'm here. Walk around the yard."

"I've been trying to be more spontaneous—like you—and less *planful* all the time. More open to experience. But maybe that's just not for me," said Patsy. She began walking a big circle in front of the shed, like she was picketing it. From the far end, she called, "I tried it with my sermon last week and it was a disaster. I had it all worked out in my head, and I decided to deliver it without notes. But I completely froze up. Fortunately there weren't that many people there, and when I realized I'd forgotten what I wanted to say, I just started them on a hymn." Patsy began humming, then sang, quite tunefully, as she approached me, "*We are a gentle, angry people . . .*"

Startled by her sudden performance, I said, "That's a hymn? 'Gentle angry'? Isn't that a contradiction?"

"It's women's music—I'm surprised you don't know it," she said. "And aren't we all full of contradictions?" She sat down and pretzeled her legs into a lotus position. "I'm hoping that as the body grows more flexible, the mind will follow," she explained.

"Stay like that," I said.

"I'll try. After a while though my hips give out."

"Tell me how you became a minister," I said, hoping the answer was complicated enough to give me time to draw her pose. "It seems like you're more of a Buddhist or something."

"Quick version or real?"

"Real, of course."

"I'll give you both," said Patsy. "The quick answer is—oh, I like studying ethics and theology, and I didn't want to be a college professor. I wanted to be out in the world, helping people. And that's all true, but on top of that, I was *called*."

"You actually heard something?" I said.

"I did," said Patsy proudly. "I was a very conventional person—not like you, with your art. I got married after college. I worked while my husband went to law school.

"It was my birthday—September—and I told him that to celebrate, I wanted to go for a hike. We both loved nature; it was something we shared, so we decided to climb Mount Monadnock, up in New Hampshire. It was a weekday, so not too crowded, and nice and sunny, just a few leaves starting to turn. I got to the top before Bruce—he wasn't in as good shape as me—and he was wandering around the summit taking pictures or something. I was enjoying the view—and I heard a voice. At first I thought it was just Bruce, complaining that now we were going to have to hike all the way down over the rocks—except it didn't sound like him. And it wasn't exactly a voice . . ." She trailed off into silence, and I drew her sitting on the ground, her head bowed.

She looked up. "Even now, all these years later, after everything that's happened, it makes my skin crawl to remember it. You might think an encounter like that, out of the blue, just when you were sick and tired of appeasing your crabby husband and writing his law school papers, would be a joyful event—but it wasn't at all. It was scary and creepy. Of course I thought I was going crazy—hearing a voice. And I must've yelled something back at it, because Bruce came rushing over and made me sit down on a log and eat some of his Raisinets, to get my strength back."

"So, what was it? What did it say?"

"That's something I've never revealed to anyone, Nora."

"And that's that?" I put down my pencil.

"I mean, I would, but I can't put it into words that anyone else would understand. And it's never happened again, either—thank goodness!"

"But—that's a totally disappointing explanation! How does hearing a voice after hiking up some huge mountain translate into 'be a minister'?"

"A small mountain, really. That's why it's usually so crowded. And it's so strange; it wasn't at all, that day." She unraveled her legs. "Sorry, I can't keep sitting like that." She stood and began pacing again. "Who knows? Maybe what I thought was a call was just dehydration," she admitted. "It took me years to interpret it. It wasn't literal—'be a minister.' It was more like validation that I could become a competent and caring person. That I could lead—" She caught herself. "Wrong word, too hierarchical. I could *encourage* the people up the mountain, where it's calm and beautiful. I'd never believed I was capable of something like that—but that was the message.

"So anyway, when we got home Bruce had made a coconut cake—I remember that, because he wasn't usually a baker—and he kissed me and lit birthday candles. And I became fascinated with the little flames dancing around. 'Blow them out already!' he said, and I did, but then I began to light candles for all kinds of occasions, and to do rituals—started going to a women's new moon circle. Things like that.

"Bruce thought I was wasting my time, and he got annoyed. But I told him I wanted—needed—to go to divinity school, and even though we'd decided to separate by then, he said he'd pay my tuition, just like I'd paid his. He's a great believer in fairness, even if he is a dork. So our split was pretty amicable—I still talk to his mom all the time.

"I know I'm not the perfect minister—but mostly the people in the congregation like me, and I've been able to offer them help or at least comfort in their difficult times. And I'm always trying, always learning. So I think I got the call right—I truly love this profession, in a way I never thought would be possible, back in those married days.

"And you know something else? I've never eaten another Raisinet. Not even at the movies." She stopped pacing and hugged herself. "It's getting cold out here. Can we stop now and go inside?"

"It'll be freezing in there too," I said, packing up my pencils and paper. "I'll put these away, and then let's go to Spiritus. We can sit inside and order a vegan pie."

"My favorite," said Patsy.

The Swim

A few days before the swim, Baby and I were finishing our morning coffee, and I was about to gather my things together to leave for my shift when Baby said, "By the way, I told Broony I'd stay over at her place the night before the Swim." She was attempting her usual casualness.

"Oh," I said. I had assumed she had spent nights with Broony before, but now it seemed that the sleepover was unprecedented, and a big deal. I wished she hadn't mentioned it.

"You can understand, sweetie, can't you? It's special for Broony," she added in a rush. "After all our training together." At least with me, Baby had never been susceptible to pressure or guilt. I wondered how Broony had done it, and if it meant their thing was turning into something else. A relationship.

"I'll try," I said, choking out the words. I cleared my throat. "I'll try," I said again, louder than I had intended.

Baby reached across the table and took my hand. "You're the best," she said and gave my hand a tug. "Come here."

"But aren't you athletes supposed to refrain before a match?" I asked hopefully.

Baby laughed, as though I had told a joke. "Oh you. Don't be silly; that's an old wives' tale."

I stood, and she caught me around the waist and pulled me into her lap. She began teasing my earlobe with her tongue, and as I relaxed into her arms, she murmured, "When the swim is over, I will devote myself to you. Promise." She gave my lobe a final nip, pushed me off her lap, looked me up and down. "I can't wait," she said.

But if she was so eager to be with me, then why oh why was she messing around with Broony? I reminded myself that it was simply her nature, which I should emulate, and live more as she did—appreciate her when we were together, and not worry about what she was doing, or who she was with, when we weren't.

Fat chance, though. For the next few days, I worked, made dinner for Miss Ruby and me, and took advantage of the lengthening days to walk in the evenings. No matter how often I had wandered any particular side street, there always seemed to be a quaint little house that I had never noticed, its lighted windows warm and inviting. Many had so little frontage that I could see into the living rooms, to couples watching TV together on the couch or sharing a glass of wine. I always ended my walk at the bay, where I took off my shoes and dabbled my feet in the freezing water until my bones started to ache, and I felt sorry for the swimmers, until I remembered that they would all be wearing wet suits and booties, and anyhow, it served them right, two of them at least.

On the morning of the Swim, Tony pulled up in her truck, honking like mad, at about 7:00 a.m.—way before Miss Ruby liked to be roused. I went into the living room to see what was going on and found her, annoyed, wrapped in a huge terrycloth robe that according to the red crest on the lapel had apparently been stolen from the Lisbon Hilton. She yanked open the door and stuck out her head. "Quit that racket!" she yelled.

"Are you gals at it again?" someone answered her from across the street.

"Jeez, that was years ago," Miss Ruby yelled back. Tony honked a few more times and then descended from the cab. "Get in here!" Miss Ruby told her. "The Swim doesn't even start until eleven."

"I was excited," Tony said. "Couldn't sleep."

The forecast had been for a clear day, but the sky was low and gray. "It's going to rain," I commented hopefully.

"Nah," said Tony. "This kind of thing, it'll burn off by 8:30."

"I don't know, Tone," said Miss Ruby. "Nora could be right. It has that settled-in look."

"And what exactly makes you think that?" said Tony.

"My pop was a fisherman," said Miss Ruby. "I've got the instinct. You'll see."

But Tony was right. It drizzled a bit, which caused Miss Ruby to gloat, but little by little, seams opened in the cloud cover, and by the time the three of us loaded our signs into the truck and squeezed into the front seat, the sun shone brightly on a pretty Cape spring day, sparrows twittering in the trees, humans and nature alike ignoring the mourning doves' continual, ominous hooting.

I was pleased with my signs. I had decorated the "Go Baby!" sides with multicolored curly ribbons and sequins and shards of purple-streaked scallop shells that I had gathered on the beach, while the reverse, "What's Polluting Our Water?" sides were stark, black sans serif caps on white. Tony dropped off Miss Ruby and me and the signs at the Boatslip motel and bar, from which the swimmers would be ferried out to Long Point, the very tip of Cape Cod, the cupped hand that sheltered the harbor. From there they would swim the mile and a quarter back to the Boatslip, accompanied by a motley flotilla of kayaks, canoes, rowboats, and other floating devices. Tony drove away to find parking.

"Careful how you carry those," I told Miss Ruby. "I don't want everything falling off them."

"Figures Tony would get out of hauling this stuff around."

"I just hope she doesn't miss the swim looking for parking, with town being so crowded."

"You'd think it was the Season already," Miss Ruby agreed and chanted the *Jaws* music. "*Dum*-dum *dum*-dum *dum*-dum *dum*-dum."

"I bet people do that who never even saw the movie," I said. "Do you think the guy who wrote it gets good royalties?"

"Movie?" said Miss Ruby.

The Boatslip deck was busier than a tea dance on a Saturday in July, with people spilling over onto the beach in front of it, the whole area jammed with what seemed like the town's entire off-season population, chatting, yelling, waving signs and streamers and balloons. A woman was pushing through the crowd gathering up the balloons. "Don't you know these kill the fish? They get stuck in their little throats." A small child began to cry, and she handed him a lollipop. He stared at it.

"All that sugar!" his mother exclaimed. "How dare you give that to my kid! He doesn't even know what it is." She pried the lollipop from his fist, and he shrieked. People turned to look at them with disapproval. "This is her fault, not mine," the mother tried to explain, as the balloon lady wandered back into the crowd.

Swimmers with their wet suits pulled up to the waist, sleeves flapping around their thighs, were lined up at a long registration table, filling out forms. Some were using the back of an obliging friend as a writing surface, and I realized one of the pairs was Broony and Baby. Baby was facing away from me, but Broony, bent over with her hands on her knees, already completely encased in black, her raspberry forelock showing from under her wet suit's tight hood, turned her head and grinned at me. I stared back at her.

Tony tapped me on the shoulder. "Had to go all the way back to my place," she said. "Come on, let's do a ribbon." She pointed to a desk next to the registration table, where a crush of swimmers and spectators, including Miss Ruby, was writing with sharpie markers on colored ribbons and pinning them to a sort of clothesline stretched over the deck. "AIDS memorial," Tony explained. "We write messages to the people we've lost." She pushed in next to Miss Ruby, who was filling out a lavender ribbon.

Tony looked over her shoulder. "Who're you writing to?"

Miss Ruby shook her head wordlessly.

"Old flame," Tony explained to me. "Rube's a sensitive soul, doesn't get over things like we do." The woman staffing the table had an array of ribbons draped over her arm, and Tony handed her a few dollars. The woman peeled off two ribbons and gave them to Tony, and Tony passed one to me. "My treat," she said and began writing on hers. "Hey, Ruby, I'm writing mine to Cara too," she said.

Miss Ruby smiled at her. "Thanks, darlin', I appreciate it."

Tony turned to me. "Poor kid. Seemed like one day they were out dancing and partying, and the next she'd passed. A blessing, I guess. So they say." She patted Miss Ruby on the back and then gave her a long kiss that seemed more than simply comforting—*wow*, I thought. Of course they were close, but they had their history, and I had never seen any public or even private displays of that level of affection. I couldn't mull it over just then, though, because I had to do something with the ribbon Tony had handed me. I had no one to memorialize. Or at least, no one I knew well. I had been an artist in New York—how had I escaped serious bereavement? There had been a teaching colleague; a guy I had gone to art school with; a neighbor across the hall, single, with a dedicated cadre of caretaker-friends who had trooped in and out at all hours. I remembered Roger's legendary boyfriend, Paul Wong. "I'm sorry we never met, Paul," I wrote and pinned my ribbon to the line.

"Good girl," said Tony. She picked up the posters Miss Ruby had laid on the ground while she was working on her ribbon and ushered us away from the table and down to the beach. The swimmers were lining up to board the boats that would ferry them to Long Point.

"Quick! Take this!" yelled Tony, shoving one of my posters at me.

Miss Ruby was already waving hers above her head. "Yoohoo! Yoohoo! Baby!" She turned to me and exclaimed, "There she is! See? Up there with Brunhilde from the coffee shop! Put up your poster, Nora!"

I flapped it above my head, and I thought I saw Baby wave at me, although at that distance I couldn't be sure.

Tony put two fingers in her mouth and whistled. "Baby! Over here! You go, girl!" She explained, "This is great. We never have someone we know actually swimming, do we, Rube?

"Nope, we usually just cheer whoever's winning the race."

"Baby says it's not a race," I said. "It's for fun."

"Hold up your sign! Hold up your sign!" said Miss Ruby.

I waved it around again, and this time I was sure I saw Baby blow me a kiss. Then Broony did too. "Ick," I said.

There was a new commotion on the beach, and a line of queens in running shorts and pink sequined camisoles jogged to the front of the crowd. They capered around waving pink-and-white pompoms, then coalesced into an attempt at a kickline. Since they varied widely in flexibility and rhythmic competence, the effect was not so much Rockettes-like synchrony as every man for himself. A lesbian in a drum major's uniform cartwheeled across the sand in front of them to impressed applause from both the spectators and the cheerleaders, and the boat carrying the swimmers slowly pulled away from the beach to whistles and cheers. The flotilla paddled madly after it.

Later, after the Swim was all over, Baby told me what had happened between her and Broony on the boat, since it explained certain things. Apparently their night together had been a success, and they were enjoying cuddling together in the afterglow—at least, to the extent that their wet suits would allow.

Then Broony said, "I saw your girl Nora the other day."

"Well, sure," said Baby. "She's around."

"On our Green Teddy patio."

"Her and half the town," said Baby, leaning away from her. "Hey, what's this all about, Broon-Broon? Don't start getting all possessive on me; I thought you said you weren't the type."

"She doesn't tell you these things? She was with a boy and that cute black girl she used to go with!"

"Her ex. They're trying to be friends. You know how that is."

"Maybe for you friendly American dykes. For myself, I can't get used to this. She is two-timing you for sure." Broony tried to slide back into Baby's arms, but Baby stood and walked out to the bow, where she leaned over the railing and watched Long Point Light get bigger and bigger as the boat drew close to shore.

With a loud, shaking groan, the boat's engine shut off, its vibrations suddenly quiet, and the crew began ushering the swimmers down the gangplank and into the shallow water. When they had all been unloaded and lined up, one of the organizers called through a bullhorn: "On your marks! Get set! Go swimmers!" The paddlers in the flotilla cheered, and the swimmers began splashing back toward town, Baby among them, concentrating on the coordination of her strokes and her breathing and not looking around to see if Broony was with her.

Back where I was, at the Boatslip, a DJ started up some music, and the cheerleaders began dancing to the thumping beat. Surrounded by a crush of fans, the Hat Sisters, a couple of burly, mustachioed queens, made their entrance. They had created their usual towering headgear, crowned, for this occasion, with models of Long Point Light. Cameras clicked and snapped. The memorial ribbons fluttered in the breeze. Those who had thought to bring field glasses scanned the harbor, watching for the first swimmers to come in, as others crowded around them. "See anyone yet?"

"Can I take a look?"

Reverend Patsy led a group of congregants to the front of the crowd, where the cheerleaders made way for them. The DJ lowered the music. Patsy raised her arms, and the UU church choir—Margot in with the baritones—began to perform their unique arrangement of the 1960s hit "C'mon Let's Swim." The lyrics took on new meaning for the day, and I clapped along as the choir sang the chorus: "Do what you wanna, do like you wish / C'mon Baby now and swim like a fish!"

When the choir finished their version, the DJ cued up the original. The Hat Sisters did a dignified switch of the hips from side to side in time to the music while making breaststroke motions with their arms, and the cheerleaders, jumping up and down, encouraged the crowd in a wilder version of the dance. Miss Ruby grabbed my hands and Tony's, and we did the swim together in our own small circle until the song ended. Panting, Miss Ruby said, "Boy, do I remember that one." Tony nodded.

I could imagine what she meant. Junior high school slumber parties, giggly girls teaching each other the new dance steps and then—O heaven! O hell!—kissing practice, first with folded bed pillows and then with each other, as you, Future Lesbian of America, rolled away and pretended to have fallen asleep.

A spectator with binoculars pointed out the lead swimmer, making his way around the boats anchored in the harbor, and the crowd began to whistle and yell encouragement. Reaching the shallows, he stood shakily, ripped off his bright green bathing cap, and whirled it in the air. The music paused so the announcer could call out his name, and his friends ran out of the crowd to embrace him and wrap him in towels.

After that we became aware of another swimmer splashing around the moorings, and soon the harbor was dotted with scattered pairs of stroking arms. The announcer called the name of the first woman to come in. It wasn't Broony. She wasn't even second or third.

When I spotted Baby's yellow daisy bathing cap bobbing in the midst of a cluster of neon green ones, I ran down the beach, and as she staggered onto the sand I caught her in my arms. Oblivious to her clammy wet suit, I hugged her to me. "You did it!" I said. "You're fantastic!"

Baby smiled. "So glad you're here to catch me," she said, extricating herself from my arms to wave her cap above her head. "Cold, though." Her teeth were chattering.

I took her hand and led her toward the Boatslip deck. "Let's get you signed in and warmed up," I said, and she nodded. A volunteer checked off her name and sent her over to the rescue squad, which had set up inside on the dance floor. One EMT wrapped her in a foil space blanket and another handed her a Styrofoam cup of tea. She seemed somehow softer and more pliant than usual, from exhaustion, perhaps, or her mild hypothermia, and I put my arm around her shoulder in the crinkly blanket.

"So *there's* Broony," she said, pointing at a row of cots. "I wondered what happened to her."

"Weren't you swimming together?"

"We got separated," said Baby.

Feeling magnanimous, since Baby was leaning on me at the moment, I said, "I hope she's okay. Do you want to go over and talk to her, see what happened?"

"I guess so," she said. "Although I'm sure she's fine."

Broony raised her head from the cot. Her lips were as pale as her blonde hair, and even her pink forelock seemed to have faded. "I am not fine," she said and collapsed back down. "I have the *seekrankheit, mal de la mer*, whatever you want to call it."

"Seasick?" said Baby. "From swimming? After all that practicing?"

"It can happen," said Broony. "This nurse here said it can come upon one suddenly, even if never before. A girl in a rowboat picked me up. It is very humiliating, Baby, for you to see me like this. Maybe at least you can tell Nora to go away now."

But Baby seemed indifferent. "Sorry you're feeling under the weather, Broon-Broon," she said. "But it'll pass, you know. Now that you're out of the water."

"The world is still spinning," Broony whimpered, reaching for Baby's hand.

Baby ignored her. "You just need to rest." Turning to me, she said, "Let's go and watch the other swimmers coming in."

I followed her onto the deck, and we leaned on the railing over the harbor. I looked at her. "That was cold," I said. "Even *I* felt bad for her."

"This is between her and me, sweetheart," she said. "Don't worry about it. She said something, going over on the boat. Trying to make me jealous. She's getting a little too serious, you know?"

"Not like me," I said. "Skipping carefree through the flowers."

"You're different," said Baby.

"I am?" I said. Inside, I was celebrating. Broony was a loser. The laurel wreath adorned my head; the gold medal hung from my neck. Although I had always denied having a competitive streak, I wanted to

jump up and down and thrust my fists in the air and shout *woo-hoo! Yes!*
Baby wanted *me*, and I didn't care anymore about finding my friends
Miss Ruby and Tony so we could warn people about water pollution
with our posters; or looking around for Janelle, to see if she had come
out for the swim and to find out what she thought of our demonstration;
or congratulating Reverend Patsy on the choir performance; or chatting
with Margot—or anything, really, except following Baby out of the
Boatslip and down Commercial Street to her storefront, where she had
already posted a note on the door saying she was closed for the Swim,
and past the display cases, and at last into her bedroom overlooking the
harbor, where the last few swimmers were straggling in. Baby stripped
off her wet suit and pulled down the blankets on the bed; patting the
place next to her, she said, "Didn't I tell you I would devote myself to
you?"

Climbing in beside her, I said, "You did. You absolutely did."

Underneath it all I felt uncomfortable with my victory, although
not enough to renounce it. Baby had revealed a side of herself that I
hadn't seen as clearly before, although I suppose I had always known it
was there. She had been not just cold but almost ruthless, in protecting
her be-here-now flirtatiousness.

If I was a cad—and I had no doubt that I was, forsaking Janelle,
rejoicing at Broony's downfall—so was Baby.

Eyes Open

What happened to you?" asked Miss Ruby when I appeared back at our cottage late the next morning. I guess I looked somewhat disheveled. She was standing at the stove in our little kitchen, and observing her, I realized how much she had changed since we had first met. She hardly used her scooter at all anymore—mostly she saved it for trips to the Stop & Shop, and then only if she had a lot of bags to carry. She was no longer shapeless but rather impressively stout. "Want coffee?" she offered. "I just got back too, from Tony's. I'm making *Sunday brunch*!" She said it like she had invented the concept.

"Sure. What are we having?"

"Whatever I could scrounge up from the fridge. Cheese sandwiches. I cut off the moldy part. And pickles."

"Oh," I said. "I was hoping for something like French toast."

"No eggs." She handed me a mug of coffee and a sandwich on a plate, and I followed her into the living room. She settled into her chair, and I into mine across from her. "This is the life!" she said. "Sunday brunch! So where'd you go, anyway? Tony and me saw Baby at the finish line, and then you two disappeared before we put up our signs."

"Sorry," I said. "I should've been there with you."

"Never mind, we went ahead without you. And your Janelle saw us and came over to help. We had the extra sign because you weren't there, so she took that one. We didn't have a sign for her friend Mick—"

"Mi'Kay."

"That's it. That one's a long cool drink of water."

Miss Ruby too! The woman captivated everyone she encountered. "So I've been told."

166

"So she helped explain when people came over to ask us what was going on, talking about the water pollution, and how women are getting sick because of the chemicals. Her and Janelle really bonded with Tony—pulling up their shirts and comparing scars. So I invited them to dinner next week."

"What did Janelle think of that?" My triumph with Baby was starting to wear off, and I was deflating, bumping to a landing on the ground. I began to truly regret that I hadn't stuck around, after all our planning, and had missed all these interesting developments.

"She said she and Mick would love to come, Nora. She's very polite."

"Charming."

"That's it," said Miss Ruby. "Charming."

I remembered what that felt like, to be charmed by Janelle. "Hey," I said, to change the subject. "What's the story with you and Tony?"

"No story," she said, but I could see she knew exactly what I was talking about. That kiss. "She just noticed I was feeling sad."

"Oh, come on, you can tell me, of all people. I live here, remember?"

"Well," said Miss Ruby, color rising up her neck and into her cheeks.

"You're turning that Miss Ruby red! Say no more, then."

"No, I'll tell you. It's a little complicated. We used to go together."

"I know, Tony said so. When I was drawing her."

"Yeah, but did she tell you why we broke up? About her coming home every night roaring drunk and throwing me around? She might be little but she's strong. Or maybe that was the drink."

"She did tell me. But she said all that was a long time ago!"

"Not long enough. I still get nervous around her sometimes, for no real reason. It's like a flashback." She shook her head, as though to clear it. "I'm a peaceful person! I come from a peaceful home—that wasn't something I ever thought would happen in my life. *It. Was. Horrible.*" Miss Ruby banged her fist three times on the arm of her chair in time with her words. "After a while I hated myself—"

"—But why? *You* weren't doing anything wrong."

"Oh no? I threw a few good punches myself after a while. Couldn't take all that from her just lying down." She shook her head again. "You must not have ever been in that situation, Nora. It's what happens. You hate yourself, you hate her, you hate everything. Feeling that way—it's worse than the physical pain, even. Everybody was telling me to throw her out, and finally I did. I told her to get away from me. Even though she was sick, running down to Hyannis practically every day for treatments, and I could see she was a mess—heartless is what that was."

"But what else could you have done?"

"Yeah, well, there must've been something. She was always promising to reform, but I couldn't trust her. I thought I'd never trust her again." She gave a short laugh. "I probably shouldn't."

"She's different now, though, isn't she?" I said. "I mean, I can't imagine her getting violent."

Miss Ruby didn't say anything for a moment. "I know, I know, me neither. But I couldn't before! It's there, that experience. She's been trying to make up for it ever since. But I'll always hold back. So we're on, we're off. Right now, we're on. We'll probably go like that until we're too old to remember it all. Sometimes—I wish for that day.

"You live with someone, but you don't necessarily know them," Miss Ruby concluded, ominously. She stood, stacked our sandwich plates, headed into the kitchen, and I heard the water running in the sink.

I wondered what I would think about Janelle and me, or, even more difficult, Baby and me, in ten years—but I couldn't manage it, projecting myself into the future, and after a while I gave up. The present was confusing enough. I was so happy that Baby had chosen me, for now, but even through the mists of her favor I could see that I had better not ask for more. She gave what she could in the moment, and that was as far as she would go. I was walking into it, I stupidly believed, with eyes open.

A Little Rouge

Once I knew who he was, I realized Marcus did his grocery shopping quite predictably, on Wednesday afternoons. He was a person of regular habits, so Margot, his avatar, could be counted on also, to appear in front of Town Hall for an hour or so in midafternoon, weather permitting, with a longer session on summer Saturdays, as she basked in the admiration of the tourists. Lately, though, she hadn't been around.

"I miss her terribly," Marcus told me when I handed him his usual packet of a quarter pound of sliced turkey. I had been noticing, from week to week, that what had been an occasional hand tremor had become a constant vibration, and the cane he had carried from time to time was no longer an affectation but a necessity. His face had gone quite gray, and he had tried to liven it up with a little rouge, but even though he had applied it with some expertise, the effect was more garish than healthy. "I used to look forward so to her manifestations," he went on. "But now, when I open her armoire or see her sign waiting by the front door, I can't help thinking, 'What was that all about?'"

His voice was low and hoarse, so I went out from behind the counter to hear him better and took his elbow. We shuffled slowly to the cash registers. "The choral singing at our wonderful Swim seems to have put a strain on the vocal cords. I simply don't have it in me anymore."

"Maybe she'll come back when you're feeling better," I said.

Marcus smiled. "Thank you for your encouragement, Nora dear. But no, I think not, although it's been a terrific run." We stopped to wait in the checkout line, and when we got to the front, Marcus gave me a hug and an air-kiss on each cheek. "As they do in France, you know," he said. He turned away and began arranging his groceries on the belt as I watched.

I wasn't ready to leave him; in fact, I was on the verge of tears. *He's just* fatigué, I told myself, *like the day he came to the studio.*

"I'm sure you have other customers waiting," he insisted, making a brushing motion with his fingers. "Go, go, go. Back to your post!"

"See you next week, then," I said. "Or maybe I'll run into Margot on the street."

"Perhaps," said Marcus. "Perhaps."

That night, Baby noticed a lingering smudge of his rouge on my cheek, licked her finger, started to rub it off.

"No, don't," I said. "Just leave it."

Open Studio

Even if, in the middle of the night, I suspected that I was headed for a fall with Baby, in the light of day I was happy. Her renewed interest in me seemed to have released all sorts of positive energies, and I was spending time in my studio almost every day, which I felt proud of myself for, since I hadn't always been able to maintain such focus. Stop & Shop had turned out to be if not the perfect day job, then at least not a bad one, once I had bought a good pair of shoes and adjusted to being on my feet for a whole shift. It could be boring and even humiliating, with certain customers complaining about you as though you weren't standing right in front of them, but it had advantages: other customers were surprisingly appreciative, and I rarely thought about any of it when I wasn't there. In that sense, if not financially or spiritually, it was better than teaching, as I had done in the city, which could suck up as much time as I had to give it, leaving only odd hours for painting: in the middle of the night, when I would rather have been snuggled up against Janelle, or in the late afternoon, after a succession of classes and before starting dinner. Or not at all.

What had started out as one mural was turning into something more like an installation. On long sheets of paper on three sides of the studio I had painted the Provincetown environment: Earth, the grid of streets and shops and houses; Sea, the rocky shoreline and breaking waves, ducks and fishes and whales; Sky, gulls and pigeons, clouds and moon and stars, sun rising and setting. As for the portraits, some were close to finished, while others were still at the multiple sketches stage.

Still, the work hadn't completely coalesced. The thing that would pull all the pieces together was missing, or hadn't yet announced itself. I didn't mind that, though. I had gotten far enough to feel confident that eventually it would, although not far enough to know what it would be, and I was enjoying the anticipation of a surprise soon to be revealed. I hadn't attempted such a large, complicated work before, so this feeling was new, and I was interested to see what would occur to me next— although I guess my subjects were less so, having allowed me to draw them and wanting reassurance that I hadn't botched them too much. They had all asked at least occasionally when they could take a look, but their questions were starting to become more persistent. I decided to throw an open studio party, a work-in-progress kind of thing, not a substitute for an exhibit in a respectable gallery—I hadn't traveled so far from Brooklyn that I no longer saw that as my goal.

Baby turned suddenly shy about my drawings of her. In addition to the ones I had done in the studio, I had sketched her at home in her kitchen, and once or twice—quickly, before she sensed me looking at her and jumped up—sleeping. "Those are between us," she said.

"Us," I echoed. I loved her saying "us." She agreed that I could hang her portrait, one of the best I had made, with her red cowboy boots as a focal point.

Everyone I invited accepted instantly. "Finally!" said Miss Ruby. "I give you the idea to take over that shed, and suddenly it's a big mystery."

"What do you mean? It's right there; you could go over any time!"

"And barge in?" said Miss Ruby. "You'd bite my head off."

"Exactly, Rube," Tony added. She had been bustling around the house constantly, bossing Miss Ruby and defending her to me. "No *real* artist wants to be interrupted like that."

"What about that guy in the West End?" I said. He had planted a sign in his front garden that said "Yes you are welcome to come in when I am painting."

Tony made a brush-off gesture with her hand. "Phoo. He just wants to sell the tourists his overpriced seascapes. They're all the same, except the color of the sky."

"Sky's difficult," I pointed out.

"He oughta be better at it by now. He had one in the window the other day that was green. Now when did you ever see a green sunset?"

"Artistic license?" I said. "So it wasn't green, but maybe he *experienced* it as green, or saw the green highlights in the other colors. Or wanted to see what it would look like, green. You're so literal."

"That's me!" said Tony.

"Then maybe art is lost on you," I said.

"His, yeah," said Tony.

But, so what if he was painting, essentially, souvenirs, for couples to hang over the couch to remind them of their romantic summer, once the winter dark closed in and things got rough—so what if his pictures were more therapy than art? My real concern, set off by Tony, wasn't his work, but mine. I had taken liberties with my palette too, and I had gone for an expressionistic, Alice Neel–ish style.

Dabbing away in my shack, stepping back to enjoy the colors and shapes evolving on my easel, I had forgotten about the fear and shame involved in exposing my work in public—or even, as I was thinking of doing now, to a few basically friendly people. Fear and shame, yet also gratification and affirmation: If the audience connected and came to share my perceptions. If they loved me. The old masochist-narcissist seesaw.

"Well, I'm definitely going," said Miss Ruby, to disrupt Tony's teasing. She had seen the worry and regret on my face. "I want to see what you've been up to, all this time."

"Me too," said Tony. "Just trying to get your goat, Nora. Can't help it."

The studio, with its rough walls, wasn't the ideal place for an art show, but I tacked the backgrounds across the slats and the sketches and the paintings, in their various stages, on the exposed studs. The one of Baby I displayed on my easel, to look as though I had just been working on it and had walked away briefly for a break. I had picked up a nest of

TV tables at a yard sale, and Miss Ruby helped me set them up with brie and crackers, and a few bottles of white wine and seltzer and Diet Coke, just like a real art opening.

Early June is the Cape's most unpredictable month, either lashing rains or gentle sun, and I had gotten the sun—a breezy afternoon with a promise of summer, warm enough for Miss Ruby and me to sit outside to wait for my guests. I noticed that over the winter, cutting across the property line in the snow and the mud, I had tamped down a path in the lawn. I was wondering if there was a way to rake the crabgrass to cover it when a guy stepped out onto the deck of the big house next door. The summer tenants were here! This one was wearing shorts and no shirt, justifiably, since he had the abs and biceps for it, had probably worked on them all winter, becoming a fixture at his gym and resisting all carbs and fats. Now he was holding a red plastic party cup. "What up?" he yelled over the thumping music that had started up behind him. "You're trespassing, dudes."

"Nah," Miss Ruby called back. "We're allowed to use the place. How was your winter?"

"Miss Ruby!" I whispered. "That's not true!"

"Like I told you, no one cares," she hissed back.

The tenant didn't answer, just went back in, slamming the door behind him.

"Festive," said Miss Ruby. "I don't think he meant to bang the door like that."

Tony came huffing across the lawn. "Sorry," she said. She opened the studio door and looked around. "I meant to get here to help set up—but I see you've done okay without me. Sponsees, you know. They get into their scrapes and I have to sort them out."

The shed grew crowded with other guests after that: Reverend Patsy with a few of her congregants and a skinny bald guy with a straggly gray pony tail whom she introduced as her meditation teacher, then my boss and coworkers from the Stop & Shop, and Bob from the Teddy, and Chuck Pina, and Silvie from the post office, whom I hadn't invited but

who seemed to find out about and attend everything. Finally, Janelle
and Roger. With Mi'Kay. I recognized her immediately: her sharp nose
and cheekbones; kohl-lined, observant eyes; and a complicated braided
hairdo that accentuated her height.

Intimidated, I held out my hand. "Nora Griffin."

She took it, then laughed and said, "Oh, please, no formalities," and
leaned down to envelop me in a hug. "I just feel like I know you already,
Nora," she said. "Ever since I saw the beautiful portrait you made of
Janelle. But this . . ." She swept her hand around the room. "Way beyond. Awesome! Really. Such color! Such insight into character! Such
love!"

"Thanks," I said, smitten. "You really seem to understand what I'm
doing."

"Oh, absolutely," said Mi'Kay. "Excuse me, but I have to take a
closer look." She turned away from me and stood for a while gazing at
the murals, then moved on to examine the portrait of Baby—who just
at that moment appeared in person, *tak-tok-tak-ing* through the door,
red cowboy boots, purpley lipstick, rough blonde hair and all, smiling,
making a beeline for me, holding out a big bouquet of flowers. Mi'Kay
looked up, and I swear I saw a spark arc and fizz between the two of
them.

Janelle said later that she saw the same thing.

But all that was interrupted, at least for the moment, by loud
knocking. "Just come in!" I yelled. "It's open!"

The door opened on a puzzled-looking man holding a rake.

"Mr. Ruis!" said Miss Ruby, bustling over to corner him in the doorway. "It's been ages! I hear you and Gloria moved down to Chatham."

"The boys told me there was some kind of commotion going on up
here," he said. "What're you getting up to, Miss R?"

"Nothing," she said. "Really. You just stopped by at a busy time."

He stared at her. "This crazy place. Yeah we moved down Cape—
we should've got off entirely. Why you people think you can just—I
don't know, just walk in! On a man's property! I want you cleared the

hell out." He looked around at my drawings and paintings, and sniffed the turpentine in the air. "And put this place back like it was. It's a tool-shed for chrisake."

"I thought it was part of our deal, Joe," said Miss Ruby.

"What deal? We never had no kind of deal. I want you out of here," he repeated. "And the cabin, too. Our niece needs a place; I'm gonna put her in it." He handed her the rake and walked out.

The room was silent, all of us looking at Miss Ruby. "Whoa," she said. "My landlord."

"Maybe he'll forget about it," said Tony.

"Doubt it," said Miss Ruby. "Although he never seemed like the possessive type before."

"All right, all right, then let's get to work," said Tony as she clapped her hands. Somehow, she instantly had Reverend Patsy and the con-gregants and meditation teacher taking down the murals, while others started packing up my supplies and picking up paintings to carry down to Miss Ruby's cottage. "Careful with all that!" Tony said.

"It's a falling-down shed!" said Miss Ruby, still standing there in the midst of it all. "He's never had any use for it." She tossed the rake out the door, its tines boinging over the ground. "Probably never will, either. I bet he doesn't even have a niece."

"Watch it with that thing," said Tony. She turned to me. "So what're you going to do about this sorry situation, *Norma*?"

We were back to that—and I had no idea. Miss Ruby came over and put her arm around my shoulder. "Don't blame her, Tony," she said. "It was me put her up to it."

"Naturally," said Tony. "I will never understand you, Rube—why you do this stuff."

"She was helping me!" I said.

"That's how it starts," Tony told me. "You should've known."

Tony left when the other guests did, after they finished clearing out the studio. For all the time I had spent there and all the work I had done, it took almost no time for them to restore it to its original, abandoned-looking state. Soon there were just five of us sitting around glumly in Miss Ruby's living room, she in her recliner with a cat or two; Baby and me, Janelle, Roger, and Mi'Kay on the floor, finishing up the brie and crackers and drinking warm white wine from plastic cups.

"This stuff's awful," said Janelle. "I don't know why I'm drinking it."

"Bad wine's the tradition at openings," I said.

She went into the kitchen to pour it down the sink.

"Oh, Nora, your beautiful show," said Baby. "I'm so sorry it ended like this." She leaned over to kiss me, but our lips misconnected and our teeth clicked—probably because, just for a second, her eyes darted over to catch Mi'Kay's.

"Yeah," I said. I didn't think I could say more without starting to cry. Everything I had put together during the long winter seemed to be falling apart at once, and I felt like I had when Janelle had first kicked me out: stopped in my tracks. That day, Miss Ruby had appeared to pick me up, but this time she was already here.

And in a low voice, Baby was asking Mi'Kay, "Have we met before?"

"Not in this life," said Mi'Kay.

L'Heure Bleue

The bad news didn't stop with my so-called party. Marcus hadn't attended because at the time he was in an ambulance speeding down Route 6, and I hope he was unconscious. Everyone's seen those ambulances, cherry lights rotating ineffectively, stuck in traffic on the two-lane stretch between Orleans and Dennis. People called it suicide alley because of the supposed frequency of collisions, but the ambulances were the more common problem, the drivers around them pulling over onto the muddy shoulder and offering a brief prayer to whatever god or goddess they subscribed to, or just to the random universe, that the victim inside had something like a broken limb that could wait out the journey, and not a stroke or a heart attack—and sometimes the prayers worked, but not that day, not for Marcus. He didn't make it much farther than Eastham.

No one could believe he was gone, and Margot with him. I couldn't have been the only one who kept looking for her singing in front of Town Hall, especially on the nicer days, as the Cape warmed toward summer.

A son nobody had ever heard of showed up to take charge of the funeral, so the obituaries made no mention of Margot, her performances, or the pleasure she had given her audiences—but a people's memorial sprang up in front of Town Hall, a red wagon kept full of flowers and a framed photograph of Margot. Propped against the wagon was Margot's sign, "Living My Dream," and next to it a boom box softly played Sinatra. One day I gathered up my drawings and the painting I had made of Marcus and placed them among the bouquets. Sitting among the other idlers on the long benches everyone called the meat-rack, watching the daily parade on Commercial Street and sketching the passersby, I can't say I exactly felt Margot's spirit, or Marcus's, but it was comforting just to sit there as people came and went, listening to "Witchcraft" and "Strangers in the Night" and other songs I had always thought were so corny.

As the sun was setting I got up to walk through town. I left my pictures of Marcus at the memorial and headed off, away from the sun, through the East End, past houses so big they obstructed any view of the bay, most still boarded up and deserted, until I reached the point where the parallels of Commercial and Bradford Streets converged into Route 6A, and there was a platform with a set of wooden stairs that led down to the beach. I stopped at the top and leaned on the railing to look back over the crescent sweep of the bay, Provincetown silhouetted against a broad band of orange at the horizon.

A gray-haired woman in silver sneakers leading a huge black dog on a leash turned away, disappointed that they had arrived too late for a run on the beach. The beach was gone; water lapped the bottom stairs, and ducks flapped around in the shallows. I watched them fish: some species tipping into the water, pointed tails in the air, webbed feet working frantically to keep them inverted, others plunging down completely, to pop up like bathtub toys yards away.

A girl I used to date wore a perfume called L'Heure Bleue, and it came in a bottle just that deep shade of spring sky after sunset, when it's so saturated that the color runs out and stains everything, walkers bundled in sweaters against the crepuscular chill, houses, dogs, ducks, me—all indistinguishably *bleue*.

I had gotten a phone call. These things happen.

It was great news, sort of: a job offer. My dilemma was that it was at Pratt Institute, back in Brooklyn, where I used to pick up a studio class or two each semester. The school was looking to replace a painting teacher who would be going on sabbatical. So it wasn't permanent, but it was full time, the kind of thing that gets your toe in the door. With maternity leaves and other sabbaticals and sudden departures by temperamental divas, if you're good, you can become a fixture. At one time I would hardly have believed my luck, an offer like that coming out of nowhere, just as I was again losing both lover and home, unsure of where I would land.

With Baby, everything had become tears and recriminations—at least, on my part. I was definitely no fun anymore. No more worries about squares; that was smashed to bits. Baby had her moments of sadness and regret, when she would try to coax me into her bed—but it was obvious to me that these were only brief interruptions in the irrepressible exhilaration of early love. Mi'Kay was no Broony, no Nora, even. She wasn't just a thing. She was *the* thing.

"I'll never forget you," said Baby, reaching out for a final hug as I picked up my knapsack from the back of her kitchen chair, to walk out her door for the last time. I avoided her arms.

And Mr. Ruis was sticking to his threat to evict Miss Ruby. "Who needs him?" she said when she decided to move in with Tony, at least as a trial. Tony was so full of satisfaction and pride as she helped Miss Ruby pack that she went around puffed up like a little rooster—or maybe the resemblance was because of the haircut one of her sponsees had given her, high and tight, the few gray curls left on top sticking up like a comb. She and Janelle had bonded as survivors, on the day of the Swim as they held up their signs, and now they were plotting actions together. Tony was eager to chain herself to something, but Janelle no longer endorsed that sort of thing, and she sent Tony out to collect more signatures—this time, to stop the dumping of sewage in the bay. "You'd think that would be pretty basic," Janelle had said, shaking her head. "P-town. Jeez."

"You'll stay on our couch, Nora," Miss Ruby invited me. "Until we find you a place."

"That's right," said Tony. "You won't be the first to sleep on the thing."

That didn't make it attractive. I went back and forth in my mind about a million times, the college waiting for my response, Miss Ruby and Tony offering to buy a new mattress, and even Janelle trying to persuade me to stay, as we felt our way toward becoming true friends in the wake of our mutual abandonment. She was moving on, climbing out of illness and anger, recovering her sweet, outgoing nature and even picking up a few new, P-town clients for her business. But I was sad and agitated.

If nothing else though, I had the momentum of my artwork, and that evening, drenched in blue, standing at the point where the parallels converge and looking back at the town, black now against the fading sky, I thought about how you sometimes have to step away from the easel to get a useful perspective and see the whole picture, and once and for all I decided to go home.

Janelle

There was something I had to do first, though. Bob let me take over a corner of his patio one sunny day, when I reminded him that I no longer had a studio to work in—although he looked at me suspiciously when I showed up with my pads and pencils. He pulled Teddy out of his pocket and poked the toy into my knapsack. "Teddy want to know," he said in his squeaky voice. "Where spray paint?"

"Threw it away," I said. "I learned my lesson. This is something different."

"I should hope so," he said in his normal bass, replacing Teddy and going back inside.

When Janelle arrived, he bustled out again with complimentary lattes. "Brunhilde quit, if you must know," he told me when he set mine down. "Barely a day's notice. She just came in the other morning and announced that she was going back to her German girlfriend. With the season coming on and everything! I'm really pissed."

"Good riddance," I said.

"I know you girls didn't always see eye to eye," said Bob, shaking his head. "But she was a natural with the coffee machine. My best barista ever."

"Oh, come on," I said. "It can't be that hard to learn."

"You don't understand," he grumbled. "She had the touch. Very special. I don't suppose you'd consider coming back?"

"Wow, Bob, I'm honored," I said. Even though we had become friends, I had never thought he would trust me as far as that. "But I don't think I could ever take Broony's place."

When he had gone, Janelle said, "Okay, where do you want me?"

"Stay right there." I pointed at her. "Across from me. You know, find a comfortable position, and then don't wiggle around too much."

"The old routine," she said.

This wasn't the first portrait I had painted of her, after all. "Exactly," I said.

She took a sip of coffee, and I waited for her to put her cup down. "So here we are," she said. "Our big idea. Who would've thought."

"A long, strange trip," I agreed, glancing up at her, then down at my sketch pad. She looked, frankly, older and more tired than in the previous portrait I had made: her face thinner and her dimples more deeply carved, her eyes darker and more searching. Her tufts had filled in, and just recently she had bleached her hair blonde, despite her misgivings about the chemical exposure. "For summer," she said. "I can't see myself as gray just yet."

I wouldn't put her against an indoor background this time. I would paint her in front of a blue sky, with ovals of clouds, *m*-shapes among them to signify the gulls, big ones for the gulls, smaller ones for the pigeons, the way children draw them. They show each other: *This is how you make a bird.*

"I like your new hair."

"A couple of the white women in my support group told me theirs grew back curly. I thought mine might grow back straight. Cancer's so perverse."

"I wouldn't put anything past it."

"Mutation, growth, transformation—you'd think it would be something positive." She paused. "We both ended up in a mess, didn't we?"

I had intended to apologize for bringing Baby into her life, and for the way she had proceeded to rip off so much from Janelle—me, Mi'Kay. Or at least, I imagined that was how Janelle saw it. "I'm sorry—" I started.

"Don't," she said. "You're not."

"No," I said. "I guess not." I couldn't regret Baby, not yet, nor wish nothing had happened between us, and that Janelle and I were still together, and figuring out how to rebuild our lives together in Provincetown.

"She didn't even know me," said Janelle. "It wasn't personal. It's just the way she operates. Without thinking."

Caddishly, I thought. "I can see why you think she's like that," I said, resisting agreement. Baby was Baby—her own woman, with her own set of rules. "It was me, too, though."

"Oh, believe me, I'm aware of that," said Janelle. "I'm working on that." She paused. "I figured out why I like coding so much. Because with computers, you create your own little universe, and it makes sense. Zero, one. On, off. It does what you tell it. Not like this out here, with all these variables. Mi'Kay was never going to stay with me. I knew that from the start—"

"Me and Baby too! It was just supposed to be—"

"She was like one of those birds that gets caught up in a hurricane and blown off course, into some strange new environment. A parrot among the pigeons. She was getting over cancer too, remember. She needed to settle down for a while and figure out where she'd landed— and there I was."

"You have your good points," I said.

"I'm trying to figure out what they are, exactly."

"And so what if she's a parrot? All they can do is repeat what people tell them."

"And be beautiful." She leaned across the table to look at the sketch I was making. "Look how serious I am, Nora. Can't you make me look at least a little happy? We're out here together. We're trying. It's a nice day."

I tore off the sheet and started a new drawing, in which Janelle was smiling—not just at the nice day but at me, as I hoped she eventually would. "I'm going back to the city," I said.

"Roger told me."

"He said I could stay with him, until I find my own place."

"Also the lady at the post office—"

"—Sylvie—"

"She said you'd been getting a lot of fat envelopes, return address Brooklyn, because you got a big glamorous job."

"She's such a busybody! Do you think she steams the envelopes open?"

"Nah, half the time she's wrong."

"Roger thinks it's weird that lesbians stay friends with their ex-lovers," I said.

"He thinks everything lesbians do is weird," said Janelle. "He'll get over it."

Present Tense

An unexpected perk of my teaching job is that my department gives me a studio, a real one, with walls and big windows and heat and hot water in the sink. I've been making self-portraits. Even though I don't think my installation will ever all fit together perfectly, which anyway is not the point—do the patterns of a life ever become that clear?—it was persistently missing a piece. Which was: me. The artist herself. So I've gone from standing back to get a view of the whole thing to close-ups.

I mount a mirror on my easel and force myself to stare into it. At first all I see is the sagging of my cheeks and softening of my jawline, the gray in my hair: time to find a new colorist; the Moldovan girl was nice but she didn't do me any favors. I put down my brushes and get on the phone to Roger, see if he knows anyone. He'll ask around.

Stop, focus, sit back down, go deeper. I try to interpret the cryptic lines and discolorations of my mature face, and what they say about my life experience and character.

I develop a new pallet, different from the one I used for the other portraits, more primary, less subtle. Less nice and pretty. Then I abandon even that for ink wash, a medium that's supposed to capture the evanescent spirit of the thing, underneath its literal façade. I look, look, and look. What do I see? I don't know.

It's exhausting after a while, and I have work to do for my classes, so I put my art things away and go home. I have a home. I only had to stay with Roger for a month, because the daughter of a colleague at school was moving out of her apartment. It's small but sunny, and I feel lucky to have it, even though it's a fourth-floor walk-up. By now I'm so used to the stairs I don't notice them, and my calves have gotten round and hard again, like they were when I first met Janelle.

My students just handed in their midterms—I had them write papers instead of simply take an exam, so they're all mad at me. I told them it would be good practice, and they said they're artists, not writers. But, you'll have to write, I insisted. You'll be writing grants, artist's statements—let's be professional here. They don't believe me, and now I have a huge pile of essays to correct. I've given myself a quota: five a day. When I finish, I reward myself. I put on a jacket, stick my wallet in my pocket, do up the complicated Brooklyn locks on the door, run down the stairs.

There's a diner on my corner, the kind with no sign and no name, and cake stands full of pale, puffy muffins ranged along a sticky counter. Someone, sometime, must buy them. The coffee is bitter and burnt— somehow always burnt, even when the surly waitress makes a fresh pot because she sees me coming. She's got these short razored-off black bangs and red lipstick and a diamond chip in her nose, and she'll consent to walk around the block with me when she goes on break.

She could be trouble.

Afterword

This book is a novel. Any resemblance of its characters to persons living or dead is coincidental—almost. Margot's persona is based on that of the late, much-missed street performer Miss Ellie Castillo (1931–2011); Margot's character, behavior, and personal history, however, are my fabrications. To read about the real Miss Ellie, visit https://www.findagrave.com/cgi-bin/fg.cgi?page=gr&GRid=73791145.

Although the campaign against mosquito spraying that Nora organizes is fictitious, Protect Our Cape Cod Aquifer (POCCA) has worked for many years to stop the spraying of water-contaminating herbicides under power lines on the Cape by the region's electrical company, Eversource. To learn more, visit https://poccacapecod.org/.

The Silent Spring Institute has studied the elevated incidence of breast cancer on Cape Cod. View their results at http://silentspring.org /research-area/cape-cod-breast-cancer-and-environment-study. For information about black women's particular risks from breast cancer, visit http://www.sistersnetworkinc.org/breastcancerfacts.html and http://www.bwhi.org/issues-and-resources/black-women-and-breast-cancer/.

For narrative purposes, I've taken the liberty of moving the date of the annual Swim for Life from September to May. The Swim benefits Provincetown's AIDS, women's health, and community groups. To learn more or donate, visit http://swim4life.org/.

To read more about the Hat Sisters, Tim O'Connor and his husband, the late John Michael Gray, and the fabulous millinery in which they regularly appeared at fund-raisers for LGBT and AIDS organizations, and other arts and charitable nonprofits, visit http://www.therainbow timesmass.com/hat-sisters-legacy-lives-farewell-john-michael-gray/. I don't know whether they ever danced the Swim.

There's nothing amiss with the bottled water sold at the Provincetown Stop & Shop.

The Green Teddy may remind some people of Joe's Coffee—but it
really has nothing to do with it.

Provincetown, amazingly enough, is totally real.

Acknowledgments

Thanks to the artist Barbara Cohen for telling a story at a dinner party that became the seed from which this novel eventually grew—and for not minding that I used it. Thanks also to Urvashi Vaid and Kate Clinton for inviting me to dinner that night, for giving me space to write in their Provincetown home over numerous weekends, and for their endless support and encouragement.

The night I heard Barbara's story I was on my way for the first time to a residency at the Virginia Center for Creative Arts. During that residency and many since, VCCA has provided precious time and peace to conceive and work on this and other manuscripts.

A poster by the Provincetown artist Peter Clemons that depicts the waters of ocean and bay swirling around the tip of the Cape has long hung in my kitchen, and as I wrote *The Off Season*, it inspired me to think of the area's geography as circular rather than as the end of the line. So it feels just perfect to have Peter's colorful image on the cover of my book.

E. B. White wrote, "It is not often that someone comes along who is a true friend and a good writer." Like Charlotte, Anita Diamant and Stephen McCauley are both.

As editor in chief of *Women's Review of Books*, I am fortunate to have a meaningful day job, as well as awesome colleagues at the Wellesley Centers for Women—especially Ineke Ceder, who is not only a friend but also an incomparably sharp-eyed proofreader. WCW executive directors Susan McGee Bailey and Layli Maparyan have created a unique workplace that honors creative work of all kinds.

Thanks to Raphael Kadushin, my editor at the University of Wisconsin Press, who responded with such enthusiasm to my manuscript, and to the two manuscript reviewers whose kind praise and insightful comments helped me to greatly improve this novel.

Thanks to Carole DeSanti for the word *cad*.

Thanks especially to friends and colleagues Robin Becker, Richard Burns, Mary Cappello, Brian Cummings, Ruth Danon, Meg Kearney, Debbie Nadolney, Anne-Marie Oomen, Natania Rosenfeld, Betsy Smith, and Jean Walton; and to my sister, Priscilla Morrissey; my niece, Rachel Morrissey; and my parents, Sigmund and Serena Hoffman.

Although Roberta Stone is my wife, and therefore I'm thanking her last, as is traditional, she did not do any of the things wives are generally acknowledged for, like type my drafts, help with my research, or cook my meals. Yet every day she inspires me, holds me, makes me laugh, and makes me think. Love you, honey.